RIDE A CROOKED TRAIL

They were discharged Union soldiers, and they were destined to change Jason's entire life. The one with the strange eyes, the big man with the black beard, and the youth with the bloody bandage. The horrible deeds they committed marked them as three who had to be stopped. Even if they had to be tracked across the boundless West, through trailless land often covered with snow, across deep rivers and deadly Indian territory, through rampaging herds of buffalo, young Jason must hunt them down. He must learn to kill, not only to gain revenge, but to stay alive in a savage world!

RIDE A CROOKED TRAIL

Lewis B. Patten

This hardback edition 2008
by BBC Audiobooks Ltd
by arrangement with
Golden West Literary Agency

ISBN 978 1 405 68161 2

British Library Cataloguing in Publication Data available.

Printed and bound in Great Britain by
Antony Rowe Ltd., Chippenham, Wiltshire

1

The war hadn't been over more than a couple of months, and there were a lot of discharged soldiers traveling on the roads, heading home. Some of them had horses, but most were on foot. A few had money, but most were broke, begging food to keep them alive, or working for it if they could. Naturally, with thousands of men on the road, there were bound to be some who didn't mind stealing, or killing if that was what it took to get them what they wanted. Life had been cheap to these soldiers for a long, long time. Their standards weren't likely to change overnight.

The three who were destined to change my life arrived at our house along about dusk, and they walked into the yard in single file, all wearing remnants of Union uniforms. One was near Pa's age, with a beard that hadn't been trimmed for quite a while hiding most of his mouth. You could see his eyes above the beard, and they were powerful enough to make me remember them. Blue and penetrating, they seemed to look right through me as the man stopped me on my way to the barn with the cow. "Howdy, boy. You reckon we could get somethin' to eat and a place to sleep?"

I kept staring at his eyes, as fascinated as a bird is by a cat. I felt a shiver run along my spine. "You'll have to ask my pa," I finally managed to say. "He's up there at the house."

They turned and walked toward the house. The older man took the lead, followed by a big, muscular man of about twenty-five, with a black, full beard.

Following him was a kid about my age, a bloody rag tied around his head and yellow fuzz on his face.

That kid with the bloody bandage may have been what made Pa agree so readily to feed them and let them spend the night in the barn. Pa had said a hundred times during the war that kids were fighting it, kids no older than me, and I knew every time he saw a kid in uniform he thought of me and thanked God that so far I had not been called.

Pa had been in the war during the first year of it, but he'd been wounded at Bull Run, discharged, and sent back home. He still walked with a painful limp, but he had got so he could pretty well do what was needed around our farm. I was getting big, so I was able to do a lot of the heavy work, and Ma did what she could.

I watched while the older man crossed the porch and knocked on the kitchen door. I saw Ma for a minute, and then Pa came to the door and stepped outside. He listened to what the man had to say, but I could see him looking at the kid with the bloody bandage on his head. Then he was nodding and smiling, pointing toward the well, telling them where they could wash up. They walked in single file to the pump and I went into the barn to milk.

I was almost through when I heard the shot. I sat there on the one-legged stool a second, trying to figure out who would be shooting, and then I felt a stab of fear. I remembered the three Union soldiers and I remembered that the older one had been carrying a revolver in a holster at his side. I got up and ran out of the barn and headed toward the house.

I couldn't see any of the three. I had just about got to the kitchen door when I heard Ma scream. I heard the sounds of a scuffle and I knew the three men were inside.

What I did wasn't very smart but I wasn't thinking. I just knew Pa and Ma needed help. I slammed into the house, nearly tearing the screen door off its hinges as I entered.

Something hit me across the back, sending me forward and down to the floor. I knew I'd been hit by some kind of club, but I had no chance to recover, or roll, or try to fight. The club hit again, this time on the back of my head, and I tasted brass and saw bright lights, and felt like I was whirling in empty air for about half a second before everything went black.

I don't know how long I was there. When I awoke, I had the most horrible headache I had ever experienced. My head throbbed, each throb so painful that I winced. Lights flashed before my eyes. I felt like throwing up.

I tried to remember what had happened to me. Then I recalled the three discharged soldiers in Union uniforms. I got to my hands and knees and raised my head.

It was pitch black inside the house. I crawled back to the doorjamb and pulled myself up. I stayed there until things steadied, and then staggered across the kitchen toward the stove, where I knew the matches were.

Halfway across, I tripped over something lying on the floor, something that was soft and yielding. I groped with my hands and felt Pa's homespun pants and shirt. Scared, I got up again and made it to the stove. I struck a match, then found a candle and turned around.

Pa lay stretched out on the kitchen floor on his back. There was a spot of blood on the front of his shirt. I got down beside him, and holding the candle in my right hand, put my left hand on his chest. I prayed as desperately as anyone ever had, but no matter how I prayed I couldn't make out any movement in his chest. It was still. The flesh of his face was cold and I knew that he was dead.

I called, "Ma?" as I pushed myself to my feet. My head whirled and for a little bit I thought I was going to fall. When I felt steady enough, I walked across the kitchen toward the parlor door.

What I saw gave me the biggest shock of my life. I'll never forget it and I still have nightmares over it. Ma lay there naked, like a doll that had its clothes ripped off. She lay in a kind of twisted position, as if she'd just been thrown aside when they were through with her. There was blood on her face, and on her forehead was a big-swelled, bluish bruise, I suppose from the blow that finished her.

I was shivering now like it was mid-winter. My teeth were chattering. I went over to her, trying not to look, and got down on my knees and put my hand on her face. It was cold like Pa's.

I got up. The throbbing in my head was like someone had hit me another blow with the club. I made for the door. Crossing the kitchen, I fell over Pa's body for the second time. I crawled to the kitchen door, across the porch, and out into the yard before my stomach contracted and I threw up. I lost everything I had eaten, but even then it didn't stop. I had the dry heaves for what seemed like forever, and when I finally stopped I was soaked with sweat and shivering again.

I crawled away from the smell of vomit and stretched out on my back, gulping in the cool night air. The way I felt, I was sure I was going to die. I lay there waiting for it to happen. I wondered what it would feel like when I died, and I kept trying to put the sight of Pa and Ma out of my mind. The harder I tried, the worse I failed.

I had to do something, though. I had to get up and either go to town or start digging graves for them. But it was like I was frozen and couldn't move. I stayed on my back with my eyes closed and pretty soon I went to sleep.

This time it was really sleep and not unconsciousness, because I had nightmares about Ma and Pa being killed. When I woke up a second time, the sun was up, beating on my upturned face.

Instantly memory of what had happened came back to me. I didn't believe it because I didn't want to. I got up and went into the kitchen and right away I knew that it was true. Pa's body was still there. The cupboards had been emptied by the men who had killed him; they had ransacked the place. The jar where Ma had kept what little money we had lay broken on the floor. There couldn't have been more than two or three dollars in it. That was the value of Ma and Pa's lives, I thought bitterly.

For the first time, I felt myself getting mad. My head still throbbed, but I didn't feel like throwing up anymore. Anger ran through my veins, heating my body from head to toe.

Someway, the men who had killed Ma and Pa had to pay for what they'd done. I thought about the sheriff, Rufus Lear. He was a big, easygoing man who didn't move very fast. I seemed to hear what he would say. "I'm sorry about your pa and ma, Jason. Mighty sorry. I'll do all I can to get the men who did it. But there's thousands of discharged soldiers in the county, and more coming all the time. I got to tell you the chances ain't too good."

I knew then that I wanted more than Sheriff Lear's excuses. I wanted the man with the frightening, penetrating eyes. I wanted the big, bearded man with him, and the kid with the bloody bandage around his head.

With that decided in my mind, I knew I wasn't going to waste time going after Lear. But I did need to know which way the men had gone.

The dust in the yard was half an inch deep, and where it hadn't been scoured off by the wind it was pocked with footprints—mine, Ma's, Pa's, and those of the three men who had been here last night.

I knew the prints of Pa's heavy shoes and of Ma's small pointed ones, and I knew my own. It didn't take me long to pick out those of the three men. I followed them. They had gone to the barn, then to the smokehouse and the root cellar. I followed half a dozen trails that came to nothing before I finally found the one they'd made leaving. I'd expected their trail would head west and it did. The tracks were plain enough all the way to the road and beyond.

I went back. I was itching to be gone, but I couldn't leave Pa and Ma the way they were. I got a shovel out of the barn and went to the family burial plot where Grandma and Grandpa were buried, along with three babies Ma and Pa had before they had me. I began to dig as fast as I could, knowing if I stayed here too long the wind would scour those tracks from the road and I'd lose the killers' trail.

I had no idea of what I'd do even if I caught up with them. I figured, I guess, that I'd solve that problem when I came to it. Maybe I thought God was on my side and would help me when I needed it, even if he hadn't helped Ma and Pa.

It was close to eleven o'clock and I was soaked with sweat and panting hard when I finally got both graves four-feet deep. I knew the graves ought to be deeper, but I also knew more digging would take more time. I figured Pa would have wanted me to do it this way if he'd had a say.

I went into the house. I got blankets off the beds. I laid one over Ma, trying not to look at her, and then I rolled her up in it. I could lift and carry her. I took her out and laid her beside one of the graves I'd dug.

I couldn't lift Pa. I wrapped him in a blanket and dragged him out to the other grave. I went in, then, and got the big family Bible. I went out and opened it and read the first words my eyes touched. They were something like, "An eye for an eye and a tooth for a tooth," as near as I remember now. Out of all the words in the Bible I'd turned to those particular words, and I figured God was telling me what I had to do.

I read out loud for a little while, not remembering what I read. Only that one sentence burned deep into my mind. Then, shuddering as I did it, I rolled the bodies of my father and mother into their graves and began to fill them in. Finished, I poked a stick down into the soft earth at the head of each. When I'd avenged them, I'd come back and put a proper headstone up.

My father had been a captain in the Union cavalry before he was wounded, and he'd brought his long-barreled revolver home with him. It was up in the attic in an old trunk, along with some yellowed newspapers and a ragged battle flag with a tear in it made by a cannonball. The killers hadn't gone up to the attic so I knew the revolver would still be there. I went up and got it and carried it downstairs, along with the powder flask, the bullet pouch, and the percussion caps. Pa had showed me how to handle it once, so I loaded it, stuck it down in the holster, and strapped on the belt. I got a flour sack and filled it with food. I got a glass water jug.

We didn't have any horses, just one old mule that we used to pull the plow. He was loose down at the far end of the pasture. I put down my things and went after him. I rode him back. Pa had an old saddle in the barn. I saddled up the mule, tied on my things, mounted, and rode up the lane to the road.

By now it was late afternoon. Where the lane hit the road, I turned and looked back, feeling a burning behind my eyes and a lump in my throat. I wondered if I'd ever see the place again.

Then, feeling smaller and more alone than ever before in my life, I kicked the mule in the sides and rode west.

Wherever there was dust in the road, I could follow the boot tracks of the three men. In places where wind had scoured the dust away, I'd temporarily lose the trail.

I suppose if I'd known the difficulties I would encounter in trying to follow three nameless men across a thousand miles of nearly empty country, I'd have turned back right then.

But I was only sixteen years old. I'd never been more than thirty miles from home in my entire life. I had no conception of how big the country was.

I only knew the time had come for me to be a man. The dead bodies of my father and mother cried out to be avenged.

2

My name is Jason Willard. The first Willard, my great-grandfather, came over from England while the country was still a British colony. I guess each generation moved a little farther west. Pa had moved his family out here to southern Illinois, and later he'd sent for Grandma and Grandpa, who had sold their farm in western Pennsylvania. I didn't remember either one of them, because they died before I was born. Now I was going even farther west. I wondered how far I'd have to go before I caught up with the three men I was following. I wondered, too, what would happen if I lost the trail. I might never find them, and I felt that if I didn't I'd never know any real peace with myself.

It was about sundown when I found the place the three had camped. There were the remains of a fire, and some potato peelings on the ground, potatoes that had come from our cellar. That was all. I went on until it got too dark to see the tracks anymore.

I knew deep down that I'd eventually lose the trail. I was a full day behind the three, and eventually there'd be a rain or a windstorm, or else the tracks would just get covered over by other tracks. It was a cinch that if the men passed through a town their tracks would get lost in all the tracks the townsmen made.

So I concentrated on fixing in my mind what they'd looked like. I pictured them as they rode into the yard and stopped me on the way to the barn. I'd never forget that older one. Those eyes seemed to have burned a picture of the man in my memory. I made myself remember the second one, the big one with the black full beard, and the kid with the rag tied around his head. He'd had a sallow, thin face, like he'd just got out of the hospital, maybe, and his mouth had been kind of loose. He must have been a bugler, I thought, because they didn't let kids that age fight with the men.

I'd forgotten to bring matches. I took out half a loaf of stale bread the three hadn't taken because it was so hard. Ma had been saving it for crumbs. I chewed slowly so I'd get the most out of it. Afterward I drank a little water and lay down to sleep.

I had probably bitten off more than I could chew, I thought as I stared up at the millions of stars in the night sky. The three men had been in the war, and they'd kill me as readily as they'd look at me. Just seeing me would be enough to make them kill me, because I was a witness against them and could get them hanged for murdering my folks.

I finally went to sleep. When I woke up in the morning, I ate some more of the dried bread. Besides the bread, I had brought some potatoes that the three hadn't taken because they were from the year before and had sprouts in them. I had some dry beans and some dry corn I'd scraped up off the floor of the granary.

This morning, with my anger cooled and my reason taking over, I faced some hard, cold facts. The three men I was after had no worries about money or food, because they would steal whatever they needed as they went along.

On the other hand, I would either have to follow their example and become a thief, or I would have to stop here and there and work long enough to buy the things I'd need to go on.

If I'd been older, I'd have known how impossible it was for me to find the men. I'm glad I wasn't older, and I'm glad I didn't quit.

I'd done a little tracking, so it wasn't entirely new to me. I'd tracked the cow when I couldn't find her, and I'd tracked rabbits and foxes and deer whenever I crossed their trails. But I'd had no experience in telling how long ago a trail had been made. Even so, I had the feeling I was catching up with the men I was following, however slowly. For one thing, I was riding the mule and they were afoot. They'd stay afoot until they managed to steal some horses. I figured the main reason they hadn't stolen horses already was that folks will go to a heap of trouble to catch a horse thief and recover stolen horses. On top of that, possession of a stolen horse is enough to convict a man. Murder is a lot harder to prove—the victims are dead and can't testify.

There were more and more tracks in the road, the farther from home I went. Finally it got so hard to see the tracks that I had to get down and walk. Sometimes I had to get down on my hands and knees.

And as if that wasn't enough, clouds began to pile up ahead of me as the afternoon wore on. At around four o'clock, I guessed, they drifted across the sun. Not long afterward it began to rain.

The first drops sent little spurts of dust up from the road where they struck. Pretty soon the whole road was wet, and not long after that, it was just a puddle of mud, with water running in rivulets off the sides.

I was pretty well soaked by now and so was the mule. There didn't seem to be much sense in getting any wetter, so I left the road and took shelter underneath a tree.

It was the first setback of many I was to experience, but it hit me harder than any of the later ones. I had lost the trail. If I continued along this road, it was possible I'd go past the place where the three had turned off. And if I did that, I'd go on and on, getting farther away from them all the time.

Gloomily I shivered and stared out at the gray landscape and the pelting rain. Thunder rolled across the sky and bolts of lightning stabbed down through the mist. I sat there until the curtain of rain rolled on, feeling the bitter taste of defeat and not knowing what I should do next. Maybe I ought to go back, I thought, and let the sheriff handle it.

I made myself remember the way Ma had looked and I felt my anger stir again. There had to be ways of following and finding people without trailing them. This was not a heavily populated countryside, but there were farms, and small towns, and people. Someone would have seen the three. Someone would remember. All I had to do was be patient and persistent, and I'd eventually find someone who could tell me which way they'd gone.

I climbed on the mule and continued along the road. At dusk I saw a campfire off to the right. I got off the mule and led him. I was able to get pretty close without being heard because of the wet ground and underbrush. When I saw two men beside the fire that I'd never seen before, I walked on in.

The men were discharged Union soldiers and, like the three who had killed my folks, wore parts of uniforms. I could smell meat cooking in the pot and my mouth began to water. I was too proud to ask them for food but I figured there'd be no shame in taking some if they offered it.

They were friendly enough, even though they seemed to pay more attention to my mule than they did to me. I didn't notice it at the time because I had my eyes riveted to the stew pot, but I remembered later. They asked me to eat and I did. The stew was made of rabbit and had potatoes and carrots in it. I wolfed it down like I hadn't eaten for a week.

My head was aching again from the blow I'd gotten a couple of days before. I felt dizzy and light-headed, so pretty soon I unsaddled the mule, tied him on a long rope so he could graze, lay down, and went to sleep.

I must have needed sleep real bad. I didn't dream and I don't think I turned over all through the night. I didn't wake up until the sun was shining in my eyes. I sat up, rubbed my eyes, and looked around for the men and for my mule.

Men and mule were gone. So was my percussion six shooter, my food, and my water jug.

I stood there staring around me, wondering how long they'd been gone. Since daylight, I supposed. And me laying there snoring while they sneaked off with my things. I felt my face burning, but it was only partly on account of shame that I'd made it so easy for them to steal from me. The rest was anger. Anger because it didn't seem like you could trust anybody.

But anger didn't do me any good. It didn't get my mule back or my gun. It didn't make it possible for me, on foot, to overtake two men riding on my mule. I'd been robbed, I'd lost the trail of the three men, and maybe I didn't have brains enough for what I'd set out to do.

But I was learning. The hard way, maybe, but learning all the same. I made up my mind I wasn't going to make the same mistake again. I wasn't going to trust anybody again as long as I lived.

I was so occupied with my thoughts that I didn't hear the hoofbeats of a horse coming along the road. When I did hear, I turned my head.

A man had left the road and headed toward me. I thought about running and then changed my mind. There was no need to run because I didn't have anything left to steal.

He was a big man, I guessed over six feet tall. He had brown hair and a wide mustache that curled up at the ends of his mouth. When he smiled at me he showed a mouthful of teeth with gaps between them that were stained with tobacco. His voice was deep and kind of soothing as he asked, "What the hell are you doing away out here all alone?"

Well, I guessed it wouldn't hurt to tell him. The truth was, I was aching to tell somebody all the things that had happened to me. I started to talk and the words came tumbling out about how the two men last night had run off with my mule and gun and food while I was asleep.

The man said, "Here, put a foot in my stirrup and swing up behind me. You can tell me while we ride."

I looked at him suspiciously.

He said, "What you got left to steal? If I was going to steal from you, I'd first have to help you get back your things."

"Maybe that's just what you're fixin' to do."

"Maybe. But even if I do, you won't be no worse off then you are right now."

That was right, I had to admit. He kicked the stirrup toward me and I put a foot in it and swung up behind him. The horse made a couple of crow-hops and then settled down. The man kicked his ribs and he broke into a trot. I bounced up and down on his rump, but it beat walking, no matter what the gait.

He said, "I'm Jess McGee. What's your name, son?"

"Jason Willard."

"Where you headed? I mean, where was you headed when you lost your mule?"

I told him about what had happened to Ma and Pa. I told him about following the three men's trail until I lost it in the storm. He asked, "What you going to do when you catch up with them?"

"Kill 'em." I felt silly right after saying that, because it was so plainly impossible.

He let a little gentle sarcasm come out with his question, "All by yourself? And all at once?"

"Well, maybe not. I'd do it any way I could."

"What if you never find 'em? This is a big country, you know."

I hadn't really faced that question yet in my mind. I could go back, I supposed, and try to farm all by myself. But I didn't want to go back. The farm would remind me of Ma and Pa and of the fact that I hadn't avenged their deaths. I said, "The farm will keep. All I got to do is send the taxes once a year."

"Then you mean to keep trying until you find them or until you're satisfied you never will?"

"I guess that's it." I liked Jess McGee, even though I

told myself I shouldn't like or trust anyone. He didn't treat me like a snot-nosed kid. He treated me like he'd have treated another man.

He said, "Well, first thing is to get back your mule and gun."

I made up my mind that Jess McGee wasn't going to get back my mule and gun only to steal them himself. He'd have to kill me first. A little bleakly I thought that maybe that was exactly what he had in mind.

3

All day we rode along the dusty road. Mr. McGee talked easily of one thing or another, almost as if he was talking to himself. His voice was kind of soothing to me, particularly since he seldom expected me to say anything.

Several times I thought of Pa and Ma, and every time I did I'd feel my eyes burning and I'd feel like breaking down and bawling like a kid. I'd grit my teeth and make up my mind I wasn't going to, and it would help to remember what the three men's faces had been like.

We stopped for a little while at noon to rest Mr. McGee's horse and to eat some hard bread and cold meat he had in his saddlebags. I didn't want to stretch out afterward, but he said time spent resting a horse was a good investment, so I went along with it. Not that I had any other choice. Anyway, I figured I owed Mr. McGee a lot. He didn't have to make my troubles his. He didn't have to take me along with him. I remembered my vow not to trust anyone, but it was hard not to trust Mr. McGee.

After about an hour's rest, we mounted up again and rode on west. Toward evening we came over a long grassy ridge and could look down into a valley with a stream. There was a little town built along the stream. The houses were mostly white, all with smoke coming from their chimneys as the women cooked supper. The smoke lay in a blue layer close to the ground and along the stream.

Mr. McGee said, "I'll bet you we find your mule

down there. They wouldn't have figured on you getting here this fast on foot. They'd likely figure they were safe."

I could feel the blood pumping faster in my veins. The thought of coming up against the pair who had robbed me was both satisfying and frightening. I didn't figure Mr. McGee was going to fight my fight for me and I didn't know how I was going to fight it by myself. I didn't have a gun and they did. They were two and I was one.

We rode down the side of the ridge and entered town. There weren't very many people on the street, it being supper time. There was one saloon, right next to an old yellow frame hotel, and out in front of it was my mule. I said excitedly, "There he is!"

Mr. McGee said, "Let's go in and see about it." He rode up to the tie rail and I got down. Then he dismounted and tied the horse. I wanted to ask him how this was going to go and what I was supposed to do, but he didn't give me the chance. He said, "Come on," in a funny strained voice, and stepped through the open doors into the saloon.

It was naturally dark inside. The sun was down but it wasn't yet dark enough for the bartender to have lighted lamps. It was hard to see and it took me several seconds to get my eyes adjusted to the lack of light. But we didn't attract any attention.

Mr. McGee stopped just inside the door, probably to let his own eyes get used to the lack of light. Pretty soon I was able to see, and I recognized the pair who had stolen my gun and mule standing with some other men at the bar. I reached out and grabbed McGee's sleeve. "That's them!" I said excitedly. "What do you want me to do?"

He didn't answer me, and I realized he'd never intended that I should face the two alone. I felt an overpowering sense of gratitude toward this man who, although he scarcely knew me, was willing to fight my fight for me, risking his own life in the process. Later I was to understand that willingness.

Anyhow, Mr. McGee cleared his throat and said, "Who belongs to that gray mule outside?"

The two men immediately turned around. For a minute they looked scared when they saw Mr. McGee, with me standing right in back of him. They recognized me and they apparently thought I'd gotten the constable to help me recover my property. Then the fear left their faces. After all, I had no proof of ownership and it was their word against mine, two against one.

One of the men said, "We do. Why? Who wants to know?"

"I do. This boy says you stole the mule from him. Along with a six shooter that belonged to his pa."

One of the men smiled contemptuously. "Who you going to believe, mister, that rag-tag kid or us? That's our mule and this here gun is mine. I carried it all through the war."

I shrilled, "That's a lie! You stole my mule and gun while I was asleep!"

Mr. McGee said softly, "The boy ain't got no reason to lie, gents. You have. He described that mule and gun to me a day back along the road. I figure you're the liars. Jason, go fetch the constable. We'll let him sort this out."

The two men stood with their backs to the bar, like they were frozen there. I backed toward the door, scared to turn around.

The others in the saloon, not more than half a dozen, were watching what was going on. Mr. McGee said, "Jason!"

"Yes, sir." I backed toward the door as quickly as I could. But as I got close to it, the two at the bar made up their minds what they were going to do. One began sidling to the left, the other to the right, leaving an open space in between, and now I could see that they both had guns.

Mr. McGee didn't move and he didn't show, from

behind, that he was made uneasy by this new development. But I knew the danger he was in. They were splitting, knowing he couldn't shoot at both of them at once. He might get one but he couldn't possibly get both. And between them, they'd kill him.

They were now ten or twelve feet apart. Far enough. In another split second they'd draw their guns and shoot at Mr. McGee. He wouldn't have a chance.

I had reached the door. It shames me to admit it, but I thought of stepping out the door and running as fast as I could run. I was face to face with death for the first time in my life and I was so scared that my whole body felt like ice.

Then I looked from the two men to Mr. McGee. I could only see his back, but it was broad and solid. If he was afraid it surely didn't show. And I knew he was doing this for me.

There was only one thing I could do. Without giving it another thought I plunged forward toward the two men, running for this short, dark distance like I had never run in my life before. I headed straight toward the man on the right end, when I was halfway to him and saw him grab for his gun, I dived and slid like you do when you're coming in to home plate.

I slid on the sawdust floor faster and harder than I'd ever slid in a baseball game. My body struck the lower legs of the man on Mr. McGee's right.

He yelled, a high, angry curse, and then he came down on top of me, knocking the wind out of me. I lost interest in the proceedings for a minute because I was gasping, choking, trying to get air into my lungs.

I heard a shot, though, and smelled the acrid bite of powdersmoke. I managed to get one breath of air into my lungs before I realized the man who had fallen on top of me was still trying to get his gun out.

Even in the shape I was in, I knew Mr. McGee couldn't shoot at him for fear of hitting me. So I grabbed hold of his gun arm, pulled it close to me, and sank my teeth into his wrist.

He let out a howl that was half pain, half angry curse, but he let loose of the gun. Mr. McGee stepped close and clipped him smartly on the head with the barrel of his own gun. The man turned limp and I scrambled out from under him.

By now I was breathing, getting air into my starving lungs. I looked toward the place where the other man had been. He was lying on the floor. Mr. McGee saw the question in my eyes and said, "He's dead, Jason. He tried to kill me and I got him first."

I was numb. I'd spent my whole life without ever seeing anything more violent than a fist fight between boys my own age, and now, suddenly, in the last few days I'd seen three people dead by violence. It took a while for me to soak it in. But Mr. McGee said impatiently, "Jason, go get the constable."

I muttered, "Yes, sir," and ducked out the door, glad to get fresh air into my lungs, glad to be able to get away from that dark, smelly saloon. There were several people clustered in front of the saloon, wondering what was going on inside. I asked, "Where will I find the constable?"

One of them pointed up the street, and without waiting for more detailed directions, I ran that way. As it turned out, I didn't have to find the constable. He found me. He'd apparently heard the shot.

He was the biggest, fattest man I had ever seen. He wore a wide-brimmed hat, the kind you saw in pictures of cowboys. A vest stretched only halfway across his fat belly and it failed to hide the polished silver star pinned to his shirt.

I blurted, "Mr. McGee sent me for you, constable. There's been a shooting and I think a man is dead."

He turned me around with a hand on my shoulder and headed toward the saloon with me trotting, him waddling. That's the only word I can think of to describe the way he walked, swaying from side to side six inches with every step he took.

There was a lot of commotion down at the saloon,

and everybody was trying to talk at once. The constable pushed his way through the crowd and went inside. I came along behind, using his bulk to get me through.

The constable's voice was as big as the rest of him. His bellow cut through the noise inside the saloon and silenced it. "Now then, what's happened here?"

Mr. McGee told him about the two men stealing my mule and gun. He said he'd already sent me for the law when the two had decided to make a fight of it and had split to try and get him trapped in a crossfire. The constable listened to Mr. McGee and to others who told the same story. Once in a while he muttered something about how glad he'd be when all the damn soldiers got home and quit making trouble for everyone.

Finally he seemed satisfied. He had the dead man carried away to the undertaker's. He collared the other one, who was conscious now, and marched him off to jail. As he was leaving, Mr. McGee asked, "What about this boy's property, constable?"

Irritably the constable asked, "Which gun is his?"

I told him the one the dead man had been carrying, the one now dangling in its holster and belt from the constable's big, fat hand. The constable handed it to me. "The mule's outside. But don't you two try leavin', now. I need you for witnesses at the trial."

I started to say something, but Mr. McGee gripped my shoulder hard and I closed my mouth. The constable disappeared out the door and the bartender said, "Drinks on me, boys. One time around." He knew he'd sell plenty of drinks tonight because everyone wanted to talk about what had happened.

My head was aching something terrible, and while I didn't remember it, I supposed I'd got hit on the head again during the scuffle with the man who had fallen on top of me.

When I got a chance I whispered to Mr. McGee,

"We can't stay here an' be witnesses. Them men that killed Ma and Pa will get away."

He shushed me and turned to ask the men next to him whether he'd seen the three strangers I'd described to him in the last few days. The man nodded, and when Mr. McGee asked which way they'd gone, he said west along the main road out of town.

We stood there at the bar for a couple of hours until the bartender said it was time to close. Then we went out. Mr. McGee seemed to have made friends with everyone. They called good-bye to him and finally the last of them disappeared. There was still a light in the constable's office at the upper end of the street. Mr. McGee untied his horse and I untied my mule and we led them down the street toward the livery barn. But when we came to it, Mr. McGee just went on past. And as soon as we reached the edge of town, we mounted and rode west.

Without a witness against him, the man the constable had taken to jail would probably be released. That didn't matter to me one way or the other. I had my mule and gun back, everything except the provisions the two men had taken from me, but they didn't amount to much.

We didn't stop until the sky began to turn gray in the east. Then, as he swung stiffly from the saddle, Mr. McGee said, "We'll sleep 'til noon, Jason. I don't figure that constable is going to follow us this far."

I was glad enough to stop. My head was killing me. Flashing colored lights kept appearing before my eyes. I felt dizzy and weak. When I lay down, the world seemed to tip and whirl.

I wished I was back home in my own bed. But I wasn't going back. I closed my eyes and went to sleep.

I had terrible dreams, about Ma and Pa lying dead and their killer standing over them, blue eyes blazing like ice on fire and a smoking gun in his hand. He was raising the gun and pointing it at me, and I knew I was going to die.

I woke up with some kind of cry to find Mr. McGee standing there looking down at me. I thought it was lucky he hadn't been of a mind to steal from me, because I surely had made it easy for him if he had.

He asked me if I was up to going on and I said I was. That was a lie, but I'd made up my mind it was time for me to quit being a kid and be a man. I got up, saddled my mule, and climbed up on his back. I followed Mr. McGee down the long, winding, dusty road.

4

I've found out since that time how hard it is to read a man's character right away. People learn to show others only what they want them to see, and those things are always favorable. In some ways, it's like trying to sell or trade a horse. You don't tell what's wrong with him. You only talk about what's right.

Mr. McGee was like that with me, and I suppose with everyone else he met. He only let me know the things about him that made him look good. He hid everything else. But when you're with someone twenty-four hours a day, sooner or later it all comes out. In bits and pieces, maybe, over a long period of time. But it comes out.

I came close to worshiping Mr. McGee at first. I was sixteen years old and my folks had suddenly been taken away from me. Mr. McGee had come along and filled the empty place their loss had left. He had been good to me and had helped me, even risking his own life in the process. It wasn't any wonder that I hero-worshiped him. If he had flaws that were apparent, I didn't see them because I didn't want to see. As soon as I found out he wasn't going to steal my mule and gun, I gave him my trust.

But I also knew something else. I couldn't always count on Mr. McGee to fight my battles for me. I had set out to avenge my folks. I was going to have to equip myself to do it by myself. That meant learning to use my father's gun. More than that, it meant learning to be a man instead of a boy. Because no matter how well a boy uses a gun, he is still a boy. Only a man can stand up to men and expect to win.

I didn't even wonder what Mr. McGee's background was. I accepted him for exactly what he seemed to be. And when, that night in camp, he offered to teach me something about using my father's gun, I accepted eagerly.

We had very little powder—only a handful of bullets and caps—so to begin with, Mr. McGee taught me how to handle the gun, how to get it quickly out of its holster, how to bring it up, how to thumb back the hammer and fire it. He said, "Dueling is against the law now, Jason, but that don't mean men are going to put their guns away. I don't figure the law is ready to tell a man he can't defend himself."

I was thinking in terms of what I'd do when I caught up with the three who had killed my folks. I asked, "So what can they do?"

"Well, they'll still duel, only there'll be a difference. No face slapping. No seconds. No meeting at dawn and pacing off the distance. No formality. They'll meet face to face and they'll both grab their guns at the same time. When it's over, the man that's still alive will claim he shot in self-defense. The law can't challenge it, because there will be witnesses to back him up." Mr. McGee's eyes had a strange glow to them, as if the prospect of fighting such a duel excited him.

In a sense, he had already fought such a duel, and the law had exonerated him. I didn't see what else they could have done, but I suppose the way the law reacted to a killing might depend on who was killed.

The days that followed are confused in my memory. They seemed to blend together. We kept traveling west, through a series of small Missouri towns and settlements. Each time we reached a town, we inquired after the three men we were following. Always they were a day, or a day and a half ahead, apparently traveling unhurriedly, not knowing they were pursued. It's doubtful if they'd have hurried even if they had known because they were three and we were only two.

Each night, and sometimes when we'd stop at noon, I'd practice getting my gun out and firing it. Mr. McGee practiced with me and his own speed improved as a result. I was still only thumbing back the hammer and snapping the action of the empty gun, but all the time I was gaining confidence, because already I was nearly as fast as Mr. McGee. Many times he said, "Jason, you're a natural. You're damned near as fast as me already, and you've only been practicing for a couple of weeks." When he said that I flushed with pride and made up my mind I'd be even better than I already was.

I began to practice all by myself, when I was away from camp gathering wood or when I had wandered away from camp to relieve myself. The rusty blue finish wore off my father's gun, and the steel got bright from wear on the sides of the barrel and cylinder. The walnut grips became smooth and shiny from my hands. The holster became worn and smooth, so that the gun slipped out more easily.

But we began to encounter difficulties. At each fork in the road we would have to decide which road we were going to take. Sometimes it was easy because one of the forks would go plainly west, the other north or south. Sometimes, though, we couldn't tell which of the two forks went west, and therefore couldn't know which fork the three men had taken.

I'd take one and Mr. McGee the other. We'd push our mounts as hard as we dared until we reached a farm or settlement, until we discovered whether the three had come that way. Then one of us would have to ride back to the forks, hurry and join the other one. Each such diversion cost us hours. Sometimes it cost us half a day. The distance between us and the three we were following increased until, after a month on the trail, they were four days ahead, and they had horses now, although we didn't know where they got them or how.

It seemed like we were bound to lose them eventually but I made up my mind I wasn't going to give up. Nights, when Mr. McGee would halt to camp, I'd say, "Can't we go on for a little while? We ain't going to sleep right away anyhow. We might as well be traveling."

He'd look at me, and he'd see what was in my eyes, and most times he'd nod. "All right. Walking a few more miles ain't likely to hurt either my horse or your mule." And we'd go on until it was almost time to sleep. Then we'd camp, unsaddle and picket the horses where the grass was good. We'd eat, more times than not cold food, and we'd lie down and sleep.

I was always up before dawn. I'd get horse and mule in and saddle them. If there was water near, I'd fill Mr. McGee's canteen and the one he'd bought for me. I'd build a fire, make coffee, and, as the sky began to turn faintly gray, I'd wake Mr. McGee. By the time the sun came up we'd be on our way.

Nearly a month after I left home, we passed through Springfield, the biggest town we'd passed through yet. Knowing it would take some time to find out if the three had passed through here, we split up. Mr. McGee took the saloons because I was too young to be allowed inside. I took the other stores, the livery stables, and general merchandise stores. We agreed to meet when it got dark in front of the bank.

The first place I stopped was a small general merchandise store. It was called Hunnicutt's General Store, and sat by itself in the middle of the block with a weed-grown vacant lot on each side of it.

A bell tinkled as I opened the door. The smell inside the store was like that of every other general store I had ever been in. By no means unpleasant, it was a combination of aromas—of cloth, leather, coffee, tobacco smoke, and a lot of others I couldn't separate. I stood just inside the door and pretty soon a girl came toward me up the long aisle that ran down the middle of the store.

She was tall for a girl, though not as tall as me. She was nearly as slim as a boy, but it would have been difficult for anyone to mistake her for a boy.

I took off my hat, for some reason feeling flustered under the steady gaze of those unflustered greenish eyes. I said, "I'm Jason Willard, ma'am. I'm looking for three men and I wondered if you'd seen them in the last few days."

It was a while before she spoke. She just stood there studying me, and all the time I got more flustered. I'm sure my face turned red. Finally she asked. "What did they look like?" Her voice was soft. Certainly I'd never heard one prettier.

I said, "The older one had eyes you'd never forget. They seemed to go right through you. The second was maybe twenty-five, with a black beard, and the third was not much older than me. Last time I saw him he had a bloody rag tied around his head but that's probably gone by now."

She nodded. "I saw them. Three days ago. They came in here to buy supplies. Why are you following them?"

I'd been asked that question before and I'd always lied or just passed the question off without answering. Somehow or other, now, I wanted to stay a while and talk to this girl. I said, "They killed my ma and pa."

Her expression changed instantly. From one of cool appraisal, it changed to one of compassion and regret. "How terrible!" She stood there in shocked silence a moment and then she asked, "What will you do if you catch up with them?"

I nearly said, "Kill them," but I stopped myself in time. I wanted this girl to think well of me and I sensed that she would not think well of someone who bragged that they were going to kill someone else. I said, "Try and see that they pay for what they done."

"You're sure they did it?"

"Yes, ma'am. I'm sure. I was there. They hit me on the head and left me for dead."

"That's awful! Wouldn't the sheriff go after them?"

"I didn't ask." I grinned faintly. "It wouldn't have been any use."

"You didn't even try?"

"It wouldn't have been any use. All the sheriff in our county is good for is serving papers and sitting in front of the jail with his feet up on the rail. By the time he got around to organizing a posse, those three would have been a hundred miles away."

"You're chasing them all by yourself?"

"No, ma'am. There's a man with me. Mr. McGee. He's helping me."

"Is he a relative?"

"No, ma'am."

A grimace touched her face. "For heaven's sake, don't call me 'ma'am.' I'm not even as old as you."

"Yes, ma' . . ." I stopped. "All right. No, Mr. McGee isn't a relative."

"Then, why is he helping you? Have you known him a long time?"

I shook my head. "He just happened to come along when I needed him." Saying it out loud, it didn't sound very logical, even to me. Why *had* Mr. McGee thrown his lot in with mine? He didn't owe me anything. He wasn't a relative or even a friend. At least he hadn't been at the start.

So far, his money had financed us. He'd risked his life to recover my stolen property, and he must know he would have to risk it again when we caught up with the men we were following. I said, "I don't know why he's helping me."

She smiled faintly. "Then you had better find out, Mr. Jason Willard, before it is too late."

I nodded. Troubled by the question she had raised, I asked, "What about you? Do you work here or does your family own the store?"

"Both." She smiled. "My father owns the store but he is selling it. We are going to San Francisco." Her smile faded. "My father is not well. He wants to see the ocean before he . . . before it is too late."

I said, "I'm sorry." It sounded lame and inadequate, but I meant it and she knew I did.

"Thank you." Her smile returned. "I wish you luck."

"I do too. I mean, I wish you luck."

"Thank you."

That was all there was. I wanted to stay, and I think she wanted me to stay, but there wasn't anything else to talk about and we couldn't just stand there looking at each other. I mumbled, "Well, I got to go. Thanks for the information."

"You're welcome, Jason."

"You didn't tell me your name."

"It's Amy. Amy Hunnicutt."

I said, "Good-bye." I didn't want to go, and her eyes clung to mine in a way that told me she didn't want me to. I got as far as the door and then I turned. "How soon are you going? To San Francisco, I mean?"

"As soon as we can. Perhaps in a month."

"Maybe I'll see you again sometime."

"I hope so, Jason." Her voice was very soft.

I turned and went out into the street. I'd only seen Amy Hunnicutt for a few minutes and I'd only spoken a dozen or so words to her, but she'd had a profound effect on me. She had, in half a dozen words, made me question Mr. McGee's motives as I had never questioned them before. She'd made me want to stay here and see more of her.

Sixteen I might be, but I was as big as most men. I'd matured a lot since my parents had been killed. I was neither too young nor too immature to fall in love.

I told myself angrily that nobody falls in love in just a few minutes' time. You have to know somebody well before you fall in love with them.

Except that I felt like I'd known Amy Hunnicutt for years. And for the first time since leaving home I wondered if I was doing right.

5

Missouri was one of the border states, bitterly divided before, during, and after the war. Guerrillas had raided through Missouri during the war and there had been much destruction and loss of life. Now, afterward, the old animosities lived on.

Understandably, many Missourians did not welcome the influx of discharged Union soldiers, and often their bitterness plainly showed.

I don't know how we got as far through Missouri as we did before Mr. McGee got into trouble. But at a small town near the Missouri-Kansas line his streak of luck ran out.

He had gone into a saloon on the muddy main street of the town. It had been raining for a couple of days, a slow drizzle that turned roads and fields into seas of mud. Because I wasn't old enough to go inside, I waited outside for Mr. McGee.

We had made a soggy camp at the edge of town in a grove of trees. We had picketed the horses where there was grass. We had tried to build a fire without success. Every stick of dead wood was soaked. Finally, in chilled disgust, Mr. McGee had said he was going to town for a drink.

I went with him because I didn't want to sit in camp alone. Besides, I wanted to inquire about the three men we were following. We slogged up the muddy main street afoot, and at the first saloon, Mr. McGee turned in. There were benches on the boardwalk on both sides of the door. I sat down on one of them.

The sun was setting in the west, peeking through beneath the layer of heavy overcast. I thought that tomorrow would probably be fair. I picked up a stick and began scraping the mud off my boots. I'd get them muddy again as soon as I stepped off the walk, but it gave me something to do.

I thought about Amy Hunnicutt and wondered if I'd ever see her again. It didn't seem likely. She would be heading for San Francisco on the stagecoach. I would continue searching for the three men who had killed my folks.

I could hear the voices inside the saloon, but except for an occasional word or two, could not make out what was being said, mostly because everybody was talking at once.

But, out of the jumble of voices, I suddenly heard the raised voices of two quarreling men. I recognized one voice as that of Mr. McGee.

Not surprisingly, the argument was about the war. Mr. McGee contemptuously called the other man a rebel who ought to have been hanged, and reminded him that Union troops had whipped the hell out of the Confederates.

All the other voices inside the saloon suddenly were stilled. The silence following Mr. McGee's shouted insult was complete.

I had gotten to my feet. I stepped over in front of the doors and tried to see inside.

A few lamps had been lighted, but with the light of the dying sun lingering outside, I couldn't see anything.

Somehow or other, though, I knew what the next sound had to be. Mr. McGee had bawled a deadly insult to some Southern sympathizer, and if the man had a gun he would have to use it. I put my hand on my own gun and then let it drop away. Even if I'd been able to help Mr. McGee, I couldn't interfere. He wouldn't tolerate it and neither would anybody else.

All I could do was wait. I backed along the boardwalk to the corner of the building so that I wouldn't stop a stray bullet coming through one of the windows or the door.

It was very sudden, and shocking, for all that I expected it. Inside the saloon, two guns roared almost simultaneously, and then one of them roared a second and a third time. A bluish layer of powdersmoke drifted out over the tops of the louvered swinging doors. For an instant there was an awful silence when it didn't seem that anyone even breathed. Then a babel of voices broke out and several men burst through the swinging doors and ran up the street.

Smoking gun in hand, Mr. McGee stepped out onto the walk. He stood there for an instant before he shoved the gun into its holster at his side.

My relief at seeing him still alive disappeared almost instantly, crowded aside by wild and growing anger. Over a stupid argument he had ruined any chance I might have had of catching the men who had killed my folks. He'd be arrested for the killing in the saloon and we'd be stuck here for weeks. By the time we were able to travel again, if we ever were, the three men we were following would have disappeared.

I opened my mouth to tell him what I thought of him for getting into such a stupid and unnecessary quarrel. I didn't get a chance to say anything. Someone came diving through the doors, hit him in the back of the legs, and knocked him forward, sprawling, into the muddy street. Before Mr. McGee could recover, half a dozen men were on him, kicking, swinging fists. One had the leg of a chair and hit Mr. McGee with it several times before I quite realized the danger he was in.

Once I realized it, I didn't hesitate. My gun was loaded and had percussion caps on the nipples. It would fire. I yanked it from its holster, thumbed back the hammer, and fired it. At the sound, all motion in the street halted for an instant, and in that silence I bawled, "Get away from him!"

Sullenly they got to their feet, covered with mud.

They shuffled away from Mr. McGee, giving him a chance to rise. I could see the almost ungovernable fury in his eyes. I believe if his hands hadn't been covered with mud he'd have tried to draw and use his gun. As it was, he only swore, savagely, bitterly.

A group of men was hurrying down the street. One of them wore a lawman's badge. They reached Mr. McGee. I put my gun back into its holster as they did. The constable reached down and took Mr. McGee's muddy gun from its holster. He took Mr. McGee's arm. "This way."

Mr. McGee said, "It was self-defense! Ask anyone!"

"We'll let the judge decide that. Come on, now." The constable cocked Mr. McGee's gun. I didn't know whether it would fire or not, covered with mud the way it was, but I wasn't willing to take the chance it wouldn't and I don't think Mr. McGee was either. He looked at me, then preceded the lawman along the boardwalk toward the jail farther up the street. I followed, so angry that right then I could have shot Mr. McGee myself.

Damn him, I thought. Damn him! The war was over and arguments about it weren't going to change anything. A block up the street, Mr. McGee turned his head and looked back to see if I was following. His eyes told me he expected something from me and I knew what it was. Under my breath I cursed him again.

I glared at him and I saw his expression change to one of uncertainty. He didn't know whether I was going to help him or not. Damn him, let him worry about that for a while. Let him wonder. Anyhow, what the hell could I do?

The courthouse was a big sandstone building set right in the middle of a square block of land. There was supposed to be lawn around it, but for lack of water the grass had turned brown and was mostly worn away. Weeds had flourished in it, but now even the weeds were dead.

The jail was in the basement of the courthouse,

entered by means of a door to one side and below the main stairway leading up to the courthouse doors. The constable disappeared with Mr. McGee. Townsmen, turned back, gathered in a knot to discuss what had happened and what was going to happen to Mr. McGee.

They didn't know me and didn't know I was with Mr. McGee. I stood on the fringe of the crowd, listening to their talk and wondering what I was going to do. From the outset it was pretty plain that Mr. McGee's idea of getting cleared on account of he was just defending himself wasn't going to work here. I could tell that by listening to the talk. Just the fact that he was an ex-Yankee soldier was enough to condemn him in this town, where from the looks of things Southern sympathizers outnumbered the Northerners at least five to one.

The jury that decided his fate would be taken from the population at random. That meant it would have to be composed of ten Southerners against maybe two Northerners. Maybe they were going to bring Mr. McGee to trial, properly. But the outcome would be anything but proper. A legal lynching was what it was going to be.

But how could I help, even if I wanted to? I might be pretty good at yanking an empty gun from the holster and snapping it, but I was still not yet seventeen. I'd never fired at a man. I couldn't go blasting into the jail, and I didn't see any other way.

Listening to the people talk, I gathered that the dead man had not been the most liked man in town, but now that he was dead, people began discovering good qualities about him they hadn't noticed before. Besides that, Mr. McGee, who had killed him, was an outsider and an ex-bluebelly trooper to boot.

I stayed out of sight in the darkness, listening, until it got late and the men began drifting away to head for home. Finally nobody was left in front of the courthouse steps. I could see a light coming from the jail window, which was heavily barred, but at ground level. Walking as carefully as I could in the dry, brittle weeds, I walked to it and got down on my hands and knees.

There was no light in the cell, but a lamp was burning on the constable's desk, and by its light I could see Mr. McGee sitting on the cot, his head down in his hands as if it ached. The constable was sitting at his desk, his back to Mr. McGee.

I took hold of the bars and wiggled them to see how strong they were. I was surprised when they moved a quarter of an inch or so. Feeling around carefully, I discovered they were loose at the bottom where the sandstone block that held them had been cracked by frost. I thought that if I had a good strong team, and a chain, I could probably yank them out.

I began to feel less discouraged. I hadn't wanted to go in the front door of the jail with a gun in my hand, because I knew that if I did there was a chance I'd end up shooting someone and making an outlaw out of myself.

I picked up a small pebble and lightly knocked on the dirty window glass with it. Mr. McGee turned his head and looked up at me. I pointed to the bars and wiggled them and he nodded as if he understood. He was still covered with mud but some of it had dried and flaked away.

I got to my feet and backed off. When I figured it was safe, I turned and ran. I went down the main street until I reached the livery barn. The place was deserted and dark. I'd made up my mind what I was going to do but that didn't mean I wasn't scared. My knees knocked together so hard I could actually hear them, and my teeth were chattering.

First, we had to have a couple of saddle horses that would get us away after I broke Mr. McGee out of jail. I sneaked into the livery, knowing there might be a hostler sleeping in the tack room like there so often was.

Sure enough, the door of the tackroom was open,

and from inside I could hear a man snoring. I eased the tackroom door shut. There was a hasp on the outside, and I stuck a big spike that was hanging from a thong through it so the hostler couldn't get out even if he did happen to wake up. Then, as quietly as I could, I went back to the stalls that lined the building on both sides.

In the dark it's hard to tell good horses from bad, but I didn't think they'd have any horses in stalls that weren't good, so I took the first two I came to. Luckily there was a thick layer of dry manure on the floor so they didn't make much noise. I led them to the front of the building and out into the street. There wasn't a single light on the street, not even in the saloon.

Mr. McGee's horse and my mule were still picketed at our camp at the edge of town. I led the two horses I'd stolen there and put Mr. McGee's saddle and mine on them. I mounted one, and leading the other, rode to the courthouse by a roundabout way. I tied the two horses to a scraggly looking tree on the courthouse lawn.

I was sweating now, but I was also cold. Already I'd done enough to get me a couple of years in jail. But it was too late for going back. I made my way back to the stable. The hostler still had not waked up.

In the corral out back I located a couple of good-sized work horses, probably used for pulling freight wagons. I found some harness hanging on nails just inside the door, and hoping the harness would fit, carried it to where the horses were. The harness must have been meant for these two horses because it fit perfectly. I found a couple of singletrees and a doubletree and a piece of chain. Handling them made what sounded to me like a thunderous racket, but apparently the racket wasn't loud enough to wake the hostler up.

I headed for the courthouse again, weighed down by the heavy doubletree, chain, and singletrees, and leading the two placid horses. When I got to the courthouse I led them to the jail window and hitched them up. I wrapped the chain around the bars so the whole thing would have to come when the horses pulled. I hooked it to the doubletree. I looked in and saw Mr. McGee watching me. The constable had his feet up on his desk and it looked like he was asleep. Mr. McGee nodded at me. He took off one of his boots to use for breaking the glass out of the window once the bars were gone.

This was pretty risky for Mr. McGee. Everything depended on speed because the noise of the bars tearing loose was bound to wake the constable up. I didn't know whether he'd shoot Mr. McGee before he'd let him crawl out the window, but there was a chance he would.

Mr. McGee didn't seem to be afraid. I led the horses away from the building until the chain was tight. Then I got behind them and picked up the reins. I slapped their backs with the reins and said, "Giddap!"

They leaned into their collars. The chain creaked as it tightened. The links slipped once on the bars and then the whole thing came loose as the sandstone in which the bars were imbedded fractured. Surprisingly, it didn't make much noise. I halted the team and looked down into the window.

Mr. McGee, instead of breaking it, had opened it. He was halfway through before the constable yelled, "Hey!"

I grabbed Mr. McGee and helped pull him the rest of the way through. A gun blasted inside the jail, but Mr. McGee was up and running after me toward where the stolen saddle horses were tied, carrying one boot in his hand.

We had reached them and mounted before the constable came bursting out of the door, carrying the lamp. Blinded as he was by the light, he never saw us at all. He just heard the beat of the horses' hooves as we galloped along the darkened street and out of town.

We were outlaws now, wanted for murder and for horse stealing. But in spite of knowing that, I couldn't help feeling pretty satisfied with myself. I had undertaken a man's job and had brought it off. Better still, I had squared accounts with Mr. McGee. I didn't owe him a damn thing anymore.

6

We rode the two stolen horses hard for about half an hour. They were eager to run so we didn't check them until several miles lay between us and the town. Then Mr. McGee slowed his horse to a walk and I followed suit. He said, "Well now, Jason Willard, that was a pretty good jailbreak for a sixteen-year-old kid."

He was talking down to me and I didn't like it, but I didn't say anything. It upset me that my feeling of friendship toward Mr. McGee was deteriorating. At first he had seemed to be a man who could do no wrong. Now I could see flaws in everything he did.

He tried again. "They'd have convicted me sure as hell."

I said sourly, "I should have let them. You didn't have to get into that fight and you didn't have to kill that man. What were you trying to prove?"

Mr. McGee's voice became angrily defensive. "Prove? I don't have to prove anything! It was an argument, that's all. One that ended in a fight."

I could see that arguing with him wasn't going to accomplish anything. Besides, in a way, he was right. It had simply been an argument that ended in a fight. I didn't know for sure that he had started it and I didn't know if he had forced the fight. I only suspected it.

I said sullenly, "We're both outlaws now. You're wanted for murder and I'm wanted for jailbreak and stealing horses. We'll both hang if we're caught. I'd suggest we quit jawing about what happened and put some more distance between us and that town."

He peered through the darkness at me. I suppose he

was trying to see what my expression was. Then, without another word, he kicked his horse and moved out again, this time at a trot.

All night we maintained the same steady gait, stopping only twice to rest and water the horses and cool their backs. At neither of these stops did Mr. McGee say anything, and I ended up feeling guilty for the things I'd said to him. That angered me even more.

At daybreak we must have been thirty or forty miles away. I was worried because we didn't know if we'd taken the same road the three men we were chasing had. If we hadn't, we'd have a hell of a time locating them again, because we didn't dare go back.

Anxious to reach a town or farm where we could inquire after them, I was glad when, in mid-morning, we spotted a small farmhouse. It sat back from the road in a narrow draw. There couldn't have been more than two or three acres of cultivated land, but there were a couple of corrals, one of which held several horses. Three loose horses were reaching over the fence into the cultivated land, trying to crop some alfalfa clumps.

We'd have ridden in anyway, but the three loose horses rang a warning bell in my mind and in Mr. McGee's. He said, "Might be they're here, Jason," and kicked his horse into a lope. I kept pace but I stayed off to one side, so if someone did start shooting from the house we wouldn't be making it any easier for them than it had to be.

All the way in I leaned low over the neck of my horse so as to make a smaller target for anyone in the house. But there were no shots. The horses in the corral bunched on the near side and stared at us. The three by the fence stopped reaching and raised their heads. Twenty or thirty red chickens ran away squawking as we thundered up to the house. Otherwise everything was still.

The door of the house was open, and on the floor inside I could see a man's legs and feet. Mr. McGee left his horse running and plunged inside. With my gun in my hand I followed him, remembering for the first time that he no longer had a gun. His was back in that town where I'd broken him out of jail.

But there was no need for guns. Not here. Inside the small farmhouse there were two dead men, a young one and an older one, probably father and son. Both had been shot in the chest, by the same vicious killers who had murdered my folks and left me for dead.

I said, "You could have been killed."

He said, "We'll be blamed for this."

I said, "You didn't have a gun. How come you went charging in like a troop of cavalry?"

There was no reason why such an innocent question should make him angry. Maybe what he was really mad about was the way I'd criticized him for getting into that last fight. Anyway his face got red and his eyes narrowed dangerously. Not wanting a quarrel with him, I turned my back. I went out and walked to the fence where the three loose horses were. Their backs still had the marks of saddles on them and I knew they were the horses the three killers had ridden here. They had stolen fresh ones and left their used-up ones behind.

Mr. McGee had gone back into the house. I returned to my horse, nervously looking back along the road as if expecting a posse to appear, even though I knew such was impossible.

Staring at that empty road, I got to thinking. I'd spent my whole life without witnessing a death. Now, in the last few weeks I'd seen six. All had been unnecessary. Ma and Pa had been killed for a few dollars and some supplies. A man had died over a stolen gun and mule. Another had been killed in an argument about the war, and these two over the difference in price between three tired horses and three fresh ones.

Life seemed suddenly to have become cheap. Maybe that was because of the war, I thought. Maybe the war had made human life dirt cheap to the men who had participated in it. Maybe when you face death every day for years you stop fearing it. Certainly the three men we were following didn't seem to be afraid of the consequences of their acts.

Mr. McGee came out of the house. He was still angry, but he was making an effort to control himself. I didn't like the way he looked at me, though. It made me uneasy and cold inside. For the first time I wondered if the time was eventually going to come when I'd have to face Mr. McGee in a fight. My glance met his for an instant and I'd have sworn the same thought crossed his mind at the same time it crossed mine. He said gruffly, "No use hanging around here. There's not much we can do for them except bury them, and we haven't got time for that. The posse will do it anyway."

"You think they'll blame us for killing them?"

"Who else?" He mounted his horse and I mounted mine and we rode out again, keeping the horses at a trot. We only stopped once, when we came to a place where dust was deep in the road and hoofprints plain. Here Mr. McGee got down and studied the prints.

Near evening we came to a small settlement. You couldn't hardly call it a town because all there was to it were half a dozen buildings spread out on both sides of the road. There was a saloon and roadhouse combined, a general store, and a livery barn. There was a feed and hardware store. The other two buildings were vacant. Back behind the buildings that lined the road were some shacks.

Mr. McGee bought a gun at the hardware store, the only revolver they had. It wasn't new. Likely some soldier had sold it for eating money. Mr. McGee paid twelve dollars for it, and for some powder and ball and percussion caps. He bought extra powder, lead, and a bullet mold for me, along with more percussion caps.

He gave them to me, and I could see by his expression that my criticism still bothered him. He was like a dog that has been struck, trying to get back into the good graces of the one who struck him. He kept trying to make conversation as we rode, but I was damned if

I was going to make it that easy for him. By killing that last man he had not only made an outlaw of himself, he had made one of me as well. And all over a stupid argument.

The miles fell behind. We got about six or eight miles from town before it got too dark to ride. We made camp in a grove of cottonwoods on the bank of a dry stream. I dug down in the sand until I struck water and watered both horses before picketing them for the night. Still unwilling to make up, I went to bed. Mr. McGee angrily wrapped himself in his own blankets and laid down to sleep.

I knew I was being childish. If I didn't like what he'd done, I was free to leave him and go my own way. But I wanted to punish him. I finally went to sleep.

In the morning, Mr. McGee was the glum one. He wouldn't speak to me and he wouldn't look at me. He saddled his horse and rode out alone, leaving me to saddle my own and catch up with him.

I finally did catch up, and rode along about a dozen yards behind. Neither of us said anything. I began to feel guiltier and guiltier but I was too stubborn to make up.

All day we rode in glum silence. Mr. McGee's neck got red and stayed that way. Whenever he glanced at me, his eyes smoldered. Half a dozen times I opened my mouth to apologize, but somehow or other I couldn't get the words to come.

At nightfall, we saw another small town ahead of us. It was full dark when we reached its outskirts. There was a small stream, and after both horses had drunk their fill, I dismounted and uncoiled the picket rope.

Mr. McGee did not dismount. He sat there in silence for several moments and finally he said, "I'm going to the saloon."

I didn't answer him. Ordinarily I would have gone in to town with him, but tonight I knew he didn't want me to. He rode into the darkness and disappeared. I made a fire. I ate some cold biscuits and washed them down with water from my canteen. Afterward, I refilled the canteen from the stream, got my blanket from behind the saddle, and lay down to sleep.

My feelings about Mr. McGee were confused. Part of me wanted to leave him, and the trail of the three men who had killed my folks, because I was beginning to sense that there was only disaster ahead for me if I remained with him on their trail. Already I was wanted for jailbreak and horse stealing. How much longer would it be before I was wanted for murder too?

The other part of me still was loyal to Mr. McGee, who after all had risked his life for me, helped me trail the killers of my folks, taught me to use a gun. That part of me said I was an ingrate, that I owed Mr. McGee more than I could ever pay.

The first part came back and argued that I didn't owe him my life, and that my life was surely the price I was going to pay if I stayed with him.

I was still awake when I heard him coming back to camp several hours later. He was muttering drunkenly to himself. He got off his horse and fell flat on his face. Cursing, he got up, took the saddle off, and dumped it on the ground. He slipped the bridle off his horse and turned him loose. I stayed where I was because I knew the horse would still be nearby in the morning. He wouldn't leave my horse, which was picketed to graze.

Mr. McGee fumbled with the saddle strings, securing his blanket roll behind his saddle. His grumbling grew louder as he looked at me, rolled up in my blankets about ten feet from the dying fire. The grumbling changed to cursing, and the cursing grew louder because I neither moved nor replied.

I was actually too scared to reply. Mr. McGee's tone was quarrelsome. He was drunk enough so that he wasn't in control of himself. All day he had ridden in glum silence, with his anger growing steadily.

I wasn't used to drunks. My father had never been drunk in his life, so far as I knew. Mr. McGee was the only drunken man I'd ever seen up close.

I must have jumped a foot when Mr. McGee bawled suddenly, "Jason! Damn you, roll out of there!"

I couldn't ignore that shout. I sat up and peered at him. The fire made enough light for me to see him clearly, even if I couldn't see exactly what his expression was.

He roared, "Damn you, get your gun. I've taken all I'm going to take off you, you stinkin' snot-nosed kid. Get your gun and we'll settle this right now!"

The time I had feared had come. He was standing spread-legged on the other side of the fire with his hand hovering over the grips of his holstered gun. He was either going to kill me or I was going to kill him. Either eventuality was totally unacceptable to me. I said, "You're drunk. Go to sleep and we'll talk about it tomorrow."

His voice was a drunken bellow now, "Damn you, I am not drunk! I was never more sober in my life! I'm goin' to kill you, boy! I'm goin' to kill you no matter how damn good you think you are!"

I didn't see how I was going to get out of it. He just wasn't going to let me out of it. I threw the blanket off and reached for my boots. I said, "Let me put on my boots."

He stood there swaying. In his condition I doubted if he could hit me even if I stood still and let him empty his gun at me. On the other hand, I didn't see how I could avoid killing him. I got my boots on and reached for my gun and belt. I said, "Wait until I get the damn thing buckled on."

"I'll wait, you little sonofabitch."

I buckled on the gunbelt. I took a stance like his, facing him. I said, "All right." I still didn't know what I was going to do. Killing him in his present condition would be murder. The thought of it revolted me, but I knew I couldn't just stand there and let him murder me.

He grabbed for his gun. I didn't will it to, but my hand went to my gun automatically. It was out, and up, before Mr. McGee's gun cleared the hoster.

He staggered, off balance from the sudden violent effort of grabbing his gun. I held my fire. He staggered sideways for half a dozen feet and then collapsed to the ground, his gun still in its holster.

I holstered mine. I went to his saddle and finished untying his blanket roll. I shook the blanket out and covered him. I took off my gun and belt, then sat down and pulled off my boots.

I lay down and covered myself, listening to Mr. McGee's drunken snores. More than ever, now, I wanted to get away from him. If I did not, I would kill him or he would kill me. There could be no other end.

7

The following morning, Mr. McGee showed no sign that he remembered what had happened the night before. His eyes were red, his hands shook, and his face was grayish green. Twice he dismounted and stumbled off into the brush to vomit. He avoided my eyes, trying to give the appearance of having forgotten his run-in with me.

We left Missouri in the afternoon and rode into Kansas, with no indication that we had crossed the border except for a small, weatherbeaten sign at the side of the road. The next day, McGee had recovered, but still he avoided my eyes as much as possible. It was plain that he was ashamed. It was equally plain that he was defiant, justifying his behavior on the grounds of my misbehavior.

In the days that followed he stopped instructing me in the use of the gun, but I did not stop practicing. Many times, as I practiced, I told myself I was not doing so because I knew eventually I would have to face Mr. McGee. But I knew otherwise. The three men we still were following were now less the cause of my concern that was Mr. McGee. Drunk, he had challenged me. Eventually he would challenge me again, perhaps sober when he did. I had to be ready. I told myself that if I became fast enough and deadly enough he wouldn't challenge me at all. Nobody is fool enough to commit suicide.

So a wary truce existed between the two of us. But the fact that I was traveling on Mr. McGee's generosity rankled me increasingly. I wanted to stop, and work, and support myself. I couldn't, because if I did I would lose the trail of the men I was following.

Sometimes they got well ahead of us, by as much as a week. Other times we caught up until, on one occasion, we were less than a day behind.

Change came to me so gradually that I was hardly aware of it. My skin, already brown and weathered from sun and wind, became more so. I grew taller, perhaps because it was time for me to start shooting up. But I filled out, too. I could tell because of the way my shirt grew tight across the chest and back.

Once we had left the populated eastern part of Kansas, we came to open rolling plains. Their vastness was overwhelming, mile after mile of grassland, where ripe grass rippled in the wind like the golden waves of some gigantic sea.

This was Indian country, and we began to travel with more care. We were particular where we camped, and only had a fire if we were in a spot where dry gulch or cutbank would conceal its glow.

The road had long since deteriorated into a trail, two tracks made by the iron-tired wheels of wagons, winding away over countless hills until it disappeared in the distance.

Sometimes, now, we were able to find the tracks of the men we were following. Often enough, at least, to reassure me we had not lost the trail. Finally, about a hundred miles from the Colorado border, we came upon the wide, beaten trail of a herd of cattle going north.

We halted our horses and stared at it, wondering how many cattle it took to make a trail so broad. The grass, for a swath a quarter mile wide, had been eaten right down to the ground. Hooves had pounded what was left into dust. We scouted around for a few minutes until we picked up the tracks of the three men we were following. Instead of continuing straight west across the beaten trail of the cattle herd, they had turned into it, their tracks mingling with those of the drovers. Maybe they sensed opportunity in this enormous cattle herd, I thought.

The sun was down. We followed the trail of the herd for about a mile, looking for a good place to camp.

It was almost dark when I heard a faint shout from off to the left on the far side of the wide and beaten trail. I stopped my horse. "Hear that?"

"Hear what?"

The shout came again. I said, "There's someone over there."

Mr. McGee said, "All right. Wait here a few minutes and then ride toward the sound. I'll circle around and come up behind."

He disappeared into the gathering dusk. I sat my horse, motionless. The shout came again, and this time words were distinguishable. "Hey! Help! I'm over here!"

I knew it could be one of the three we were following. Having become aware of our pursuit, they might have set a trap for us. I didn't answer, even though the shouts continued, taking on a pain-filled, pleading note. Finally, when I guessed Mr. McGee had had time to circle around, I rode toward the sound.

My hand rested on my right thigh, only inches from the grips of my gun. I wasn't afraid but I was nervous, wondering who the man could be, wondering if, at last, I had overtaken one of the killers I was following.

Nearly all the light had by now faded from the sky. I couldn't see more than fifteen or twenty feet ahead. What I did see was blurred by darkness and hardly distinguishable as to form.

But the voice was closer now. "Thank God," it said fervently. "Thank God!"

I asked, "Who are you and what are you doing here?"

I could now make out the blurred form of a man lying on the ground. A warning chill ran along my spine. I dismounted and put my horse between the man and myself and repeated my question.

The voice from the darkness said tremulously, "I'm Frank Deacon. I got busted up when my horse fell on me and those sonsabitches left me behind to die."

I saw Mr. McGee's shape behind the prostrate man. Mr. McGee was walking, leading his horse. Mr. McGee said, "It's all right, Jason. He's alone."

I stepped from behind my horse and approached the man. It seemed barbarous to me that they would leave a man to die this way. On the other hand, reason told me they probably had no way to take the man along with them. We'd seen no wagon tracks, and if the man was as broken up as he said, he obviously couldn't ride.

We squatted down beside the injured man. He seemed starved for talk, and for a while we just let him pour it out. Finally Mr. McGee said, "Jason, see if you can find some dry buffalo chips. We'll have a fire and see what we can do for him."

I wandered out into the darkness, leaving the cattle trail. I gathered up an armload of dry buffalo chips, trying not to think about the bugs on the underside.

When my arms were loaded, I returned, and dumped the buffalo chips on the ground. I brushed my clothes anxiously with my hands, trying to get rid of the bugs. Mr. McGee lighted a fire. It burned with more blue flame than yellow, but it gave off enough light for us to see Frank Deacon.

He was a skinny man, about five feet eight. He looked to be between forty and fifty years old, but it is possible he looked older because of the pain that had drawn his face and turned his skin almost gray. His eyes squinted against the light. He wore a week's growth of whiskers. His hair hadn't seen a barber's shears for months and was a kind of mousy color, black sprinkled liberally with gray.

I said, "Three men joined this drive a mile or so back. What did they look like?"

"You know them three?"

"We think we know them. What did they look like?"

"Well, the oldest one had funny eyes. They. . . ."

I said, "I know. What about the others?"

"One was maybe twenty-five. Black hair and beard. The third one was just a kid. Kind of sallow skin."

I said, "That's them."

"What did they do?"

"Killed my folks. Left me for dead."

"How long you been followin' 'em?"

"From Illinois."

The man whistled. He shifted position. His face twisted with pain and he sucked in his breath. I asked, "Where are you hurt?"

Slowly and carefully he shook his head. "Don't know exactly. My back hurts like hell. So does the right side of me." He began wheezing, his face twisting with pain as he did. A trickle of blood appeared at the corner of his mouth.

I couldn't stand watching him. I said, "I'll get more chips." I got up from my hunkered position and hurried away.

I didn't need anybody to tell me that Frank Deacon didn't have long to live. I also knew that, the way he was busted up, it would have been barbarous for the drovers to take him along with the cattle drive. Riding horseback would have been an agony for him that he wouldn't have been able to stand for more than a few hundred yards. Riding in a wagon, even if one had been available, wouldn't have been much better. Not on the prairie, where the ground was much rougher than any road.

But they could have stayed with him until he died. I gathered up another load of buffalo chips and carried them back to the fire. Mr. McGee was sitting across the fire from Deacon. He had the coffee pot on. He also had a skillet on, with bacon in it, with cold biscuits waiting to be fried in the grease.

He had rolled a smoke for Frank Deacon. Deacon was smoking it, carefully avoiding drawing the smoke very deep into his lungs because he knew the pain a fit of coughing would bring.

I stared at Mr. McGee's face with surprise that almost bordered on disbelief. It was filled with compassion for this dying man and there was a depth of pity in his eyes I had never expected to see in them.

Mr. McGee was a complicated man. He seemed constantly compelled to prove himself, to prove his manhood not only to others but to himself as well. He was capable of unfeeling brutality while he was doing so.

But he had also been good to me, making my troubles his, accompanying me on what without him would have been a fruitless pursuit of the men who had murdered my folks. He was financing that pursuit, without apparent expectation that he would ever be repaid. Now he was showing compassion for the pain and suffering of this dying man, a stranger to us both. Yet he had, while drunk, challenged me and would have tried his best to kill me if he had not first collapsed.

I stared into the bluish flames and frowned, wishing I could understand this man who had become such a big part of my life. I didn't want a confrontation with Mr. McGee. I didn't want to shoot it out with him, because I believed I would kill him if I did. He had taught me to use a gun so well that now I was better than he.

When the coffee was finished, he poured a tin cup full and took it to Frank Deacon. Deacon held it and sipped it appreciatively, his eyes on the bacon and on the biscuits frying in the grease. I asked, "How long have you been here like this?"

"Three days."

"Without anything to eat?"

"They left me some food. I finished it yesterday."

Mr. McGee muttered something. He filled a plate with bacon and fried biscuits and took it to Deacon. Deacon's face showed so much pain when he tried to feed himself that Mr. McGee took the plate from him and began to feed him a mouthful at a time.

I helped myself from the skillet and poured myself a

cup of coffee, hardly believing what I had seen. I began to wonder what terrible thing had happened to Mr. McGee to make him the way he was. This side of him was, I guessed, the real McGee. The other side, that could kill for no reason, had to be the result of something terrible, probably something that had happened to him during the war. I wondered if I'd ever know what it was. I wasn't sure I'd ever have the courage to ask, because I sensed that asking might trigger a fury in him greater than any I had seen so far.

I finished eating. I unsaddled the horses and led them out away from the beaten cattle trail to a place where there was grass. I picketed mine and released Mr. McGee's. Carrying the two bridles, I returned to camp.

Mr. McGee was talking quietly to Frank Deacon. I got my blankets and lay down to sleep. For a while I lay awake, listening to the murmur of voices from the direction of the fire.

In the morning, Frank Deacon was dead. McGee was red-eyed from loss of sleep, and I guessed he had stayed awake all night, talking to Deacon, making his last hours of life more bearable.

We had no shovel with which to dig a grave, and there were no rocks to pile over the body. So we took Deacon to a dry wash, whose sides were steep, laid him in the bottom, then clawed earth down over him from the steep banks of the wash. Only when he was covered to a depth of a couple of feet would Mr. McGee go on.

Having seen this new side of Mr. McGee, I now found the thought of fighting him, of possibly killing him, even more unacceptable than before. Somehow I had to find a way of letting him know that a confrontation between us wasn't necessary.

Yet even as I had the thought, I doubted if it was possible.

8

So wide and plain was the trail of the herd that it could be followed even in darkness. We took a chance that the men we were following would not leave it, and rode well into the night. Both of us knew we had several days of catching up to do. But we also knew the herd was traveling slowly, probably at a rate no faster than ten or twelve miles a day. We ought to do three days' catching up tomorrow. Probably by tomorrow night we could bring it into view.

Once, I asked Mr. McGee, "How many cattle you reckon it would take to make a trail this wide?"

"Couple or three thousand, I suppose."

"Where do you think they're taking them?"

Mr. McGee shrugged. "Somebody must be starting a ranch up north of here someplace."

"In Indian country?"

He said, "Indians won't be here forever. It'll be just like it is back East. White men will eventually own it all."

I supposed that was true. I knew that our farm in Illinois had been Indian country when my grandparents came out from Pennsylvania and settled there. Now there wasn't an Indian within several hundred miles of it, and I supposed it would be no different here.

Mr. McGee seemed to have forgotten his run-in with me and I was glad he had. I didn't like there to be a strain between us. I liked to be able to talk to him.

We camped well to one side of the cattle trail where there was grass for our picketed horses to eat. But we didn't have a fire. Mr. McGee had been seeing the tracks of unshod horses all afternoon. He figured they had been made by Indian ponies, which meant Indians could be anywhere. They might even be watching us. Mr. McGee said he'd take the first watch while I slept. He woke me sometime during the night. I got up and stood watch while he lay down to sleep. Uneasy and not a little scared, I paced back and forth, my hand never far from my gun, until dawn began to streak the eastern sky.

We ate what we had cold and saddled the horses. Mr. McGee said, "Keep your eyes peeled. We don't want to get taken by surprise."

I kept looking uneasily to right and left, expecting Indians to appear on the skyline. But none did. The morning passed.

We stopped at noon to rest the horses. Mr. McGee squatted and studied cattle droppings in the trail. "Fresh." he said. "No older than half a day."

That meant the cattle herd couldn't be more than half a dozen miles ahead. I began to feel excitement because I knew that, at last, I was going to come face-to-face with the three men who had killed my folks.

I'll admit to being scared. They were three and I was only one, and I couldn't be sure Mr. McGee would help me out this time. I figured that for some obscure reason he expected to have to face me down eventually. I figured too that he knew I was faster then he was. So, why shouldn't he just let me be killed? Why should he step in when he fully expected me to kill him in the end?

Alone, I was no match for three, no matter how fast I got my gun out of its holster and fired it, no matter how accurate I was. They'd split like the two in the saloon had on Mr. McGee, so that one of them would get me no matter what I did.

I had to force myself to think of the way Pa had looked lying sprawled on the kitchen floor. I had to remember the way Ma had looked, like a stripped and naked doll somebody had thrown away.

Thinking of those things made my blood heat up and pound faster through my veins. I'd face them. Maybe I'd be killed, but I'd sure as hell take one or two of them with me when I was.

Mr. McGee was watching me. All morning he had been watching me and I knew what was in his mind. He was wondering how I'd meet the test when finally it came. He'd taught me all he could. But he couldn't teach me the thing I needed most. That had to come from inside myself.

Every time I met his glance he looked away. The fact that he did made me feel stronger and more confident. I wanted to ask him point-blank if he intended to help me. I didn't because I had no right. There was no reason on earth why he should help me, risking his own life as he did so. He didn't owe me a thing.

Yet despite all the reasonable thing I told myself, somehow I knew that when the showdown came, Mr. McGee would help. I also knew, though I don't know how, that when he did he would not be doing it for me but for himself.

For himself. How could he do it for himself? Puzzled, I rode along about fifty feet to his left, watching the horizons for Indians.

The afternoon dragged, probably because I felt the end of the trail was so very close. At last, near what I guessed was four o'clock, I saw a solitary Indian appear on the ridge ahead. He came into sight and then just sat there on his horse, not looking at us but at something in the distance.

I said hoarsely, "Look. Up there." Mr. McGee turned his head and I pointed at the Indian.

We were, at the moment, riding in the wide bed of a stream. On both sides was the wooded plain created by that stream in flood. It was heavily timbered with cottonwoods, willows, and brush, and that was the reason the Indian had not seen us before we saw him. Mr. McGee said, "Get off your horse. Tie him."

I obeyed instantly. I took cover behind the horse.

Pa's gun was in my hand, its hammer cocked. Mr. McGee looked at me and said, "For God's sake, ease that hammer down. A gunshot will bring them down on us quicker than a fox on a chicken coop."

I eased the hammer down, feeling foolish because he'd had to tell me such an elementary thing. The Indian on the ridge sat like a statue for what seemed an eternity. Then, as if he suspected he was being watched, he moved slowly out of sight behind the crest of the ridge.

I heaved a long sigh of relief. Mr. McGee waited for about five minutes to see if he would reappear. When the Indian did not, he said, "All right. Let's go."

We mounted and continued in the wide, timbered bed of the stream. After about a mile and a half, the stream took a sharp turn to the left. The cattle trail left it and climbed over a long, low ridge.

I felt naked and exposed when we left the cover of trees and brush. Mr McGee rode about fifteen feet ahead of me. I kept glancing from right to left. Once I called softly, "You ever fought Indians before?"

He swung around and looked at me. "No. Why?"

"You seem to be so sure of yourself."

That plainly pleased him. He said, "Indians can't be much different from the Johnny Rebs. They're out to kill you and you got to try and get them first."

"What do you think they'll do about that cattle herd?"

He shrugged. Having no experience with Indians, he didn't know any more about them than I did. But from what I knew about Indians, cattle didn't interest them. At least not in herds. They might want an animal or two for meat, but they wouldn't know what to do with an entire herd.

At the crest of the ridge we stopped. Staring ahead, I saw more cattle than I had ever seen before. They stretched out to right and left in a loosely held herd half a mile wide. From front to rear, the herd was almost a mile long.

Drovers were visible at the front of the herd, along

its sides, and at the rear. Absently I counted them. There was one in front, a position I later learned was called the point. There were three on each side. Two brought up the rear. The herd was moving slowly, the animals grazing placidly.

Between us and the ponderously moving herd were two groups of men. One contained maybe a dozen drovers. The other consisted of fifteen or twenty Indians. There seemed to be an argument of some kind going on.

Mr. McGee halted his horse. I stopped beside him. I asked, "What's going on?"

"Looks like they're palaverin'. Likely the Indians want some beef. Chances are the drovers don't want to give any up."

I strained my eyes trying to pick out the three men we were following. I couldn't. They were too far away. But I could see one of the white men gesturing. The Indians sat their horses stolidly.

Now, suddenly, more Indians appeared. They came over a distant ridge in a long thin line, spaced maybe forty or fifty feet apart. The line stretched away for half a mile, until the farthest Indians looked like specks. Mr. McGee whistled. "We got to help those boys," he whispered.

I asked, "Why?" thinking that those same drovers had left Frank Deacon behind to die, thinking too that the three men who had so callously murdered my pa and ma were there with them.

"What do you mean, why? They're just like us, that's why. There're up against all those damned heathen Indians."

I stared at Mr. McGee's face. It was drawn taut, the mouth thinned, the eyes narrowed. He reminded me in that instant of a dog at point or a cat stalking an unwary bird.

I said, "Maybe the drovers will give them what they want."

"By God, I hope they don't! To hell with those heathen devils!"

I said, "A couple of cows would be a small price to pay for avoiding a fight."

"Avoid a fight?" Mr. McGee seemed outraged. "Avoid a fight with these murderin' redskins?"

I said, "Why all the worry about that bunch? Didn't they leave Frank Deacon behind to die?"

"It was all they could do."

I said, "They could have stayed with him."

He groped for an answer. Finally he said, "Their boss likely decided that. You can't blame all of them for it."

I had to concede that he was right. I examined my own feelings, wondering how much of my reluctance to pitch in and help the drovers was because of what they had done, how much because I was afraid.

I had to admit, in all honesty, that much of my reluctance was because I was afraid. Then, with some defiance, I realized it was normal to be afraid. Anybody with my inexperience would be afraid. A lot of men, with experience, would be afraid. Pa had told me once that he was damn near scared to death every time he went into battle, and Pa had had lots of experience.

Why, then, wasn't Mr. McGee afraid? Why did he act like a dog on a leash, just begging to be freed?

That was a question I still had no real answer for.

9

For what seemed an eternity, all the tiny figures making up the panorama were motionless except for the line of mounted Indians moving slowly and deliberately toward the group of drovers and the score of Indians palavering with them. Several puffs of smoke came unexpectedly from the drovers' guns, and two Indians tumbled from their saddles, afterward lying motionless on the ground.

Smoke puffed instantly from the guns of the Indians as they separated themselves from the drovers. Mr McGee said with satisfaction, "Good! They didn't give the bastards anything!"

To me it looked like the worst kind of folly. A couple of steers would likely have bought peace and would have been a small price to pay. Stubbornness had caused two deaths and it had scarcely begun.

Shrill cries came from the approaching line of Indians when they saw their comrades fall. The drovers retreated hastily to a shallow draw. Dust raised in clouds from their horses' hooves as they slid down the cutbank into it. Immediately they left their saddles and scurried to the side of the draw. Puffs of smoke began coming from their guns.

I glanced at Mr. McGee. His hand, holding his bridle reins, was trembling. His eyes were glittering. He licked his lips.

Risking their lives, the Indians rode to their fallen comrades. They boosted the bodies onto horses, then quickly led the horses away. Miraculously, none was hit doing it.

I held my breath, waiting for the line of Indians to engulf the whites. The Indians apparently had other ideas. Instead of continuing toward the drovers in the draw, they turned and rode instead toward the scattered, grazing herd a quarter mile away.

Seeing them coming, men riding point, flank, and drag left their posts. One man, likely the trail boss, climbed out of the draw in which he'd taken cover and began waving his arms, plainly trying to tell them to stay where they were.

They probably didn't see. Certainly in all that confusion, they couldn't hear. Galloping their horses, they put the herd between themselves and the Indians, finally taking cover in another draw on the far side of the herd.

I glanced at Mr. McGee again. He seemed fascinated with what was going on. Sooner or later I knew he was going to have to go down and get into the fight, but at the moment he didn't seem able to tear himself away. Yelling and firing their guns, the Indians reached the uneasily stirring herd.

Ponderously the herd surged into motion. Blinding, obscuring clouds of dust arose from thousands of pounding hooves. Both Indians and cattle were, for a time, completely hidden by the dust.

Mr. McGee yelled, "Come on!" He dug heels into the horse's sides and thundered toward the dozen or so drovers who had first taken shelter in the draw. A little slow to react because of my fascination with what was happening, I finally kicked my horse and followed him, thinking not so much of helping the drovers in their fight against the Indians as of coming face-to-face with the three men we had followed for so many weeks.

Long before we reached the draw, the drovers came riding their horses out of it. They pounded away, heading toward the other draw where the men who had been holding the herd had taken refuge.

Mr. McGee and I galloped after them, about a quarter mile behind. Dust clouds drifted between us and we lost sight of them. Sometimes I even lost sight of Mr. McGee, so heavy was the dust. There was a lot of firing in the distance, and we could faintly hear the high cries of the Indians. Ahead, I suddenly saw riders pouring up out of the second draw. Galloping, yelling, both groups spurred their horses in the direction Indians and cattle herd had gone. If they saw Mr. McGee and me they gave no sign of it. I tried to pick out the three men we had been following but the dust and confusion made it impossible. Mr. McGee kicked his horse and thundered after the group and I followed him. That trail boss ought to be feeling like a prize fool by now, I thought. He'd saved a handful of steers but the cost had been his entire herd.

The dust was blinding. I let my horse have his head, knowing he could see much better than I. Distance had diminished the noise made by the Indians and I could no longer hear that peculiar rumble caused by the hooves of the stampeding cattle herd.

My horse's neck was lathered. Flecks of foam blew back and stuck to the front of my pants. I didn't know how much more our horses could stand, and I knew it was the worst kind of foolishness to kill them in this chase.

I was about ready to pull my horse to a halt when suddenly Mr. McGee and his horse appeared out of the dust cloud ahead. He had stopped. Around him were a score of other horsemen.

A big, red-faced man seemed to be in charge. In an angry, bellowing voice, he directed his men to separate into three groups. He sent one to the right, one to the left. The third group he ordered to follow the trail of the stampeding herd, picking up stragglers as they went.

Having given directions and having assigned his men, the trail boss looked at Mr. McGee and at me. "Where the hell did you come from?"

I had been glancing from face to face trying to pick out the three men we had been following. It was impossible because every man was covered with a thick layer of dust. Their eyes, mouths, and noses were rimmed with mud formed by the mixture of moisture and dust.

Mr. McGee said, "Happened onto the ruckus, is all. Thought we ought to help."

"All right," he said bruskly. "Stay with this bunch. Dollar a day and keep." He rode away.

The men in our group spread out across the broad cattle trail. I kept looking for the men we were following, without success. Finally I gave up and concentrated on the job at hand.

There were stragglers everywhere, cattle that, for one reason or another, had left the stampeding herd. By the time we had gone a mile we had gathered up more than a hundred head.

I tried to keep my mind on what we were doing but without success. All I could think was that at last I had caught up with the killers who had murdered Pa and Ma.

Only by summoning up all my outrage could I convince myself that I wasn't going to fail when the showdown came. I had never faced a man in a gun fight before, unless I considered the confrontation with Mr. McGee such a fight. I didn't know how I was going to react. But the thought of being killed scared me less than the thought that my courage might fail me when I needed it the most.

Again and again I forced myself to remember the way Ma's body had looked lying on the floor. I made myself remember my father's voice, and the way he had looked, with blood staining his shirt, his eyes open, dulled like the eyes of a dead animal. I wouldn't fail, I told myself. I couldn't fail!

Several times I caught Mr. McGee watching me. Each time I met his glance determinedly as if by doing so I could convince him I was not afraid.

But I was afraid. Fear made a tight ball of ice form in my chest until I could scarcely breathe. My hands shook. What if they shook that way when I faced the men I had followed this far?

We rode in the trail left by the stampeding herd for most of the day. Finally the trail just petered out. The men sent out on both sides came in, each driving a sizable herd of stragglers.

Then, while some of the men held the whole herd bunched, half a dozen rode into it, cutting out a thin stream of cattle, which were driven some distance away. The trail boss and two other men tallied the cattle as they left the main herd to join the second one.

With nothing particular to do, I rode from one group of men to another, looking, searching each face carefully. Mr. McGee followed me.

None of the three I sought were with the main cattle herd. I glanced at the other, smaller herd of cattle that had already been tallied. Behind me, Mr. McGee said, "They must be over there."

I nodded. Everyone was still so caked with dust that recognition was difficult. That probably explained why I had not been noticed. Besides that, the three had seen me only once and I had changed since then.

I passed within a dozen yards of the trail boss. He scowled, probably because my movement disturbed his count. One of the men with him glanced momentarily at me.

Though his face was caked with dust, those eyes were unmistakable. As blue as winter ice, they seemed to go right through me. For an instant I was back home, driving the cow across the yard to the barn, stopping in response to his inquiry about food and a place to sleep and telling him he'd have to ask my pa.

That had been the only time I'd ever seen his eyes, but they were impossible to forget. I turned my horse and rode to him.

Occupied with his count, he paid no attention to me at first. Not until I said, "You ought to remember me. I sure as hell remember you. You're the murderin' sonofabitch that killed my folks. And now I'm going to kill you."

My voice hadn't raised in pitch. It was almost quiet and it was steady, with no tremor to it. Surprisingly, I was suddenly as steady as my voice. Gone was the ball of ice inside my chest. Gone were the tremors in my hands and legs. I held my horse still less than six feet from the man.

He stopped counting and looked at me. For an instant there was genuine puzzlement in those penetrating eyes. He asked, "Who the hell *are* you?"

"It was a little farm in Illinois. You stopped me in the yard to ask if you could have something to eat and a place to sleep. I said to see my pa and you headed toward the house. Next thing I heard was a gunshot and Ma's scream. You killed them both and left me for dead. Only I wasn't dead."

I could see that he remembered now. He turned his horse slightly so that his right side was toward me, which meant he wouldn't have to bring his gun up over his horse's neck before he could fire it.

Calm and confident, I waited for him to move. I knew I could kill him. I knew I would kill him. There wasn't any doubt in my mind. I had even forgotten Mr. McGee. I didn't need Mr. McGee anymore.

With only a part of my mind, I heard the trail boss ask angrily, "What the hell is going on?"

Mr. McGee answered him. "Stay out of it. It ain't your fight."

I stared into those ice-blue eyes, waiting for the flicker that would tell me he was ready to move. And suddenly I saw a shadow of doubt in them.

But I had no time to savor it. I heard a scuffle of movement and suddenly another horse slammed hard into mine.

My horse, struck so unexpectedly, lost his footing and went down. I fell with him and my leg was pinned beneath. I had the sudden, awful fear that the man with the ice-blue eyes would kill me while I was helpless on the ground. I struggled to get my gun, which was pinned against the ground by my leg.

The trail boss's voice was furious. "Damn you, take your stinkin' quarrels someplace else! It's taken all day to gather these damn cattle up and I ain't going to have them scattered again."

I looked up, still trying to get my gun. The man with the penetrating eyes was gone. He and the other two were already a couple of hundred yards away, their horses at a lope.

My horse struggled to his feet. Released, I got up too. My leg ached, but I could walk.

I scowled at the trail boss, then swung to my horse's back. I felt like cursing him but I didn't. I was still just a kid, and, besides, I could understand why he had done what he had.

The trail boss said angrily, "Go on, get the hell out of here! Both of you!"

But I was already gone and Mr. McGee was no more than a dozen feet behind. The three we were pursuing had increased their lead to a quarter mile by now, and had disappeared over the crest of a ridge.

My inclination was to spur my horse, run him if necessary, and catch up with the three immediately. Vengeance had been in my grasp, and just as suddenly it had been yanked away.

But I resisted it. We had been following the men for weeks. Killing our horses in headlong pursuit might mean losing them once and for all.

Besides that, there were hostile Indians hereabouts. Upon our horses' strength might depend our lives.

10

It was a good thing we didn't hotly pursue the three, because we had gone no more than five miles before the pony tracks of a score of Indians turned into the trail of the three we were following. Mr. McGee said, "If we hadn't slowed down, we'd have been right in the middle of that bunch of Indians."

I said angrily, "I was so close! If it hadn't been for that damned trail boss, I'd have killed that man."

"Or he'd have killed you."

I glanced aside at him. "Is that what you think?"

"No. I think you can handle him all right. But either way, it's water over the dam. The trail boss butted in and the man got away."

The trail was headed northwest. I asked, "What's ahead? Do you know?"

"We're close to the Colorado line. I've heard about an old settlement called Julesburg Station just on the other side."

We were riding at a steady trot. I wanted to go faster but I knew doing so would be foolish. I felt a lot of frustration at the thought of the Indians catching and killing the three, because I wanted more than just to see them dead. I wanted the satisfaction of killing them myself.

I thought back to that instant of confrontation. I'd been calm and steady enough to shake the confidence of the man facing me. No longer need I doubt my own capabilities. When the time for it came, I could face the three and function the way I had been taught.

Whenever I drew abreast of him, Mr. McGee

glanced at my face and glanced away again. He had seen me face that man back there, I thought, and he had seen how I behaved. He was probably thinking ahead, to the inevitable time when he would challenge me again himself. He was wondering if he could win.

At dusk we stopped and camped. I picketed the horses while Mr. McGee went after buffalo chips and wood. I realized with surprise that things were different. Slowly, almost unnoticed by either of us, our roles had changed. No longer was he the dominant one, the teacher. No longer was I the kid, eagerly learning what he had to teach.

He returned with a load of chips and firewood, dropped it and brushed the bugs off his clothes. I knelt and built the fire. He got out the smoke-blackened pots, put some water in the coffeepot and put it on to boil. He put bacon into the other pan. Neither of us gave much thought to the fire other than to keep it as small as possible. We both figured the Indians were a long way off by now, following the three, whose names I still did not know.

As soon as the bacon had fried, he shoved it to one side of the pan. I had mixed up some flour biscuits and now I put them into the grease to fry. The coffee boiled and we hunkered down beside the fire to eat.

The bullet came out of nowhere, slamming into the fire and showering sparks over both of us. The report came hard on the heels of the bullet's impact, but we were already in motion, dropping plates and cups, diving blindly for the darkness.

I have never crawled faster on my hands and knees. Only when I was thirty feet from the fire did I stop and yank out my gun.

I crouched there silently on my knees, gun in hand, hammer thumbed back. Utter darkness surrounded me. Mr. McGee had gone the other way and now we were separated, fifty or sixty feet apart. We couldn't know whether an Indian had fired the shot, or whether the three white men had circled back to ambush us.

I turned my head, conscious of a chill crawling along my spine. Whoever had shot at us had to have seen us scramble away from the fire. He could get one of us between him and the fire, and shoot with a reasonable degree of accuracy.

The instant I realized this, I got to my feet and began to run. Blindly, recklessly, realizing to my chagrin that I was still not above feeling afraid. I circled as I ran, trying to reach Mr. McGee. If we could get together, maybe we could put up some kind of fight. This way, we were too vulnerable. Out of the darkness we could be attacked from the rear. There was little way we could defend outselves, and certainly no equality in the contest.

It occurred to me that Mr. McGee might be trying to reach me even while I was trying to reach him. I supposed it was dangerous to yell, but the attacker or attackers already knew exactly where I was. I shouted, "Mr. McGee!"

His reply came from immediately ahead. I saw his running shape too late to avoid colliding with him. We slammed together and my gun discharged accidentally. He went down and I fell on top of him.

Desperation touched me now. This was turning into a comedy of errors except that there was nothing funny in it. We were running, shouting, slamming into each other, dicharging guns accidentally. Out in the darkness were at least three, maybe a score, who had tried to kill us and would try again.

Mr. McGee grunted something disgustedly. We untangled ourselves and got up, standing back to back. I whispered. "They can silhouette us against the fire."

"Maybe. But when they do, we're going to see the flashes of their guns. We'll have something to shoot at too."

We waited, scarcely daring to breathe, listening as intently as we could for sounds. Finally I heard a faint, scuffing sound. I strained my eyes, but I couldn't see a thing.

A gun flashed. The bullet burned the side of my thigh like an iron. Almost immediately I felt the wetness of blood below the wound. I whispered. "For God's sake, the horses! This sonofabitch is pinning us down while the others steal our horses!"

Without hesitation, we both broke into a run. Straight toward the fire we ran, pounded past it and beyond to where the horses were staked out. There was a flurry of movement ahead, and suddenly figures were visible, those of horses and of men. From behind came a shout from the one assigned to keep us busy, warning that we had escaped.

A gun flashed ahead, and another, but I didn't return the fire. I was afraid of hitting one of our own horses. I crashed into a man, knocked him sprawling, and fell on top of him. I slammed my gun barrel down, drew a yell of pain from him, then broke free and scrambled to my feet again.

Dimly I glimpsed a riderless horse immediately ahead. Maybe it was mine and maybe it was not, but it was a horse and I needed one. I lunged toward it, shoved my gun barrel against the man holding the reins, and pulled the trigger. The blast of the shot was muffled by the man's body. He crumpled and I seized the horse's reins. I vaulted to his back, drummed on his flanks with my heels, and let loose a high yell that was filled with more fright than anything. Hands grabbed at my legs, but I kicked them away. One of my boots was almost yanked off, and then the horse broke into a gallop. In an instant all the yelling and confusion was behind.

There had been no time to worry about Mr. McGee. Any hesitation on my part would have resulted in my death. I looked behind, now, wondering how he had made out.

A horse was coming, maybe fifteen or twenty yards behind me and I yelled, "Mr. McGee! That you?"

"It's me!"

I kept digging the horse with my heels, because a

way behind Mr. McGee other riders were coming. After half a mile or so he drew abreast. I had no idea whether the attackers had been Indian or not but I thought they were. I yelled, "Indians?"

"Sure as hell! Six or eight of them, near as I could tell!"

"We lost our horses and all our stuff."

"We saved our hides!" I noticed now that he was also riding an Indian horse. Bareback, as I was, with a leather hackamore around the horse's nose.

We rode hard for close to half an hour. The sounds of pursuit finally died. Mr. McGee drew his Indian pony to a halt. He said, "We got our skins and we got our guns. That's better than we deserve after building a fire in Indian country."

"What are we going to do now?"

"We'll head for that settlement I told you about. We can get what we need there."

At a walk, we plodded westward. We had lost the trail of the men we were following and had no chance of finding it again. We would just have to hope they were headed for the same settlement. We didn't dare camp and sleep, because we had no way of securing the Indian ponies and didn't dare risk letting them get away.

Mr. McGee was quiet, almost glum. My attempts at conversation met with grunts. At last, in the hope of drawing him out and maybe making him feel better, I said, "Tell me about what happened to you in the war. My pa was in it for a while, until he was wounded at Bull Run."

He didn't answer me. I said, "Mr. McGee?" thinking maybe he hadn't heard.

He was riding a little ahead of me. He turned around to face me and his voice was low and angry. "Kid, that's none of your damned business!" Then, as if realizing that such intensity wasn't called for under the circumstances, he said, "It's water over the dam. I don't like to think about it, is all. I don't want to remember it!"

I was silent, startled at his response to what I had thought was a companionable request. Considering my earlier suspicions, I guess I should have known better than to bring up the subject.

But why was he so violent about refusing to talk about it? There had to be a reason.

Only one occurred to me. Mr. McGee was ashamed of something that had happened to him during the war. And I could think of only one reason for a man to be ashamed. He had failed the test. At some time or another, when courage was called for, he had shown cowardice.

I was ashamed for having had the thought. What right had I to draw such a conclusion? Mr. McGee's courage had never failed him while he was with me. Hadn't he risked his life, making my fight his own? I felt my face getting hot.

But the nagging doubt remained. If I was right, and Mr. McGee's courage had, at some time, failed him during the war, it would explain his almost fanatical compulsion continually to prove himself.

Disgustedly, I rejected that idea. It was presumptuous of me to try to explore what was in Mr. McGee's mind, let alone to make guesses that had no basis in fact. Mr. McGee had faults. Everybody did. But he had been a good friend to me. I had better concentrate on that and leave the guessing to somebody else.

11

We kept going all night. Dawn revealed empty country behind us, with no sign of telltale dust. The Indians had given up. They had our horses, saddles, and other gear. They must have been content to let it go at that.

All day we rode across the rolling, empty plain. A couple of times we saw antelope. Once we saw a dozen or so buffalo, so distant they were only black specks against the dry-brown waving grass.

In late afternoon we sighted a tree-lined river in the distance to the north. We reached it at sundown, a wide, deep river that Mr. McGee said had to be the Platte. Running beside the river was a road. We followed it, and as the last light was fading from the sky, sighed a settlement ahead.

A crudely painted sign at the edge of town announced it was Julesburg Station. Mr. McGee said we ought to leave the horses tied in the river bottom because they'd likely spook at all the noises and smells in town.

In the gray light of dusk I checked the loads in my gun. Mr. McGee followed suit. Then, side by side, we walked toward the settlement.

It could hardly be called a town. There were no more than a couple of dozen buildings in all, most of them built out of prairie sod cut in squares that had been laid up like bricks. Roofs were made from cottonwood poles laid side by side. On top of the poles was a layer of brush, and on top of that, more sod. The only lumber visible was in the doors, door frames, and window frames. Some of these were of hand-sawed and hand-hewn cottonwood. Others appeared to have been made from wagon beds.

A lot of noise was coming from one of the sod buildings. Mr. McGee said, "That one must bė a saloon." He opened the door and stepped inside.

The floor was of packed earth, covered with a thin layer of dirty sawdust and chips. There was hardly enough light inside to see the bar, but I supposed visibility would be better after our eyes got used to the lack of light. The bar was a cottonwood log sawed in two, supported by a section of cottonwood log at each end.

Warily I glanced to right and left, into the crowd. The man with the penetrating eyes hadn't recognized me when I challenged him back there with the cattle herd, but he'd recognize me now. When he did, he'd shoot me down any way he could.

We reached the bar without incident. Mr. McGee ordered whiskey. I ordered beer. It was warm and mostly foam. I'd never tasted beer before and I didn't like it. Mr. McGee put a coin on the bar, and the bartender, bearded and as dirty as any man in the saloon, made change.

The bartender lighted three more lamps, one at each end of the bar, one behind where the bottles were kept on a shelf. The added light made it possible to see into every corner of the room, and to make out the faces of all the men at the bar.

I studied each one, disappointed to discover that none of the three I was looking for was here. I beckoned the bartender, and described the three men to him. As soon as I described the eyes of the leader, he began nodding his head. "They was here," he said. "Yesterday. Ain't seen 'em today. Likely went on toward Denver."

"How far is that?"

"Hundred an' fifty, two hundred miles."

"They give their names?"

The man shook his head. "Heard 'em call that one with the funny eyes Barney."

I thanked him. Mr. McGee asked me if I wanted another beer and I said no. He poured himself another drink from the bottle the bartender had placed in front of him. He gulped it and poured a third.

I began to feel a growing uneasiness, remembering what had happened last time Mr. McGee got drunk. I thought about suggesting we leave, but I never got a chance to speak. A man on Mr. McGee's right had begun to take an interest in him and now he moved closer, peered at Mr. McGee's face and said, "By God it is you! It's Captain McGee!"

I looked at Mr. McGee's face. The light wasn't very good but it was good enough to see the way all the color had drained out of his face. It was hard to describe Mr. McGee's eyes. They had narrowed. They kept trying to look away from the stranger but something kept pulling them back.

The man turned away from Mr. McGee and spoke to the men on the other side of him. "Know who this yellow-bellied bastard is? This is Captain McGee. I was in his company during the war. Led us into an ambush, he did. Then took half the company an' ran away, leavin' the rest of us to die."

Mr. McGee said, "Jenkins, I didn't run off and leave you. We got cut off."

Jenkins' voice was contemptuous, "We was fightin' to join you, Captain. Why wasn't you fightin' to join up with us? Or at least stayin' put? Time we'd fought our way to where you'd been, you and all the others was gone. We got cut to bits, we did. Those of us that wasn't killed was taken prisoner. I spent the last six months of the war at Andersonville. Ever hear of Andersonville, you damn dirty yellow belly?"

The color suddenly returned to Mr. McGee's face. The epithet "yellow belly" made his eyes flash. His hand went toward his gun and the man said, "Go ahead! Pull your goddam gun! I'll kill you where you stand!"

I jumped away from the bar so I wouldn't be in the line of fire. Anyway, I wanted to be in position to help Mr. McGee if Jenkins' friends ganged up on him. I was in motion when the guns came out, but by the time I had taken two steps from the bar, turned, and set myself, it was over. Mr. McGee still stood in the same position, only now he held a smoking gun.

Jenkins' unfired gun hung from a hand that no longer had any strength. A red stain was spreading across the front of his dirty khaki shirt. His eyes held a look of disbelief. Then, almost deliberately, his knees buckled and he crumpled to the sawdust floor.

Mr. McGee said shrilly, "It was self-defense. He drew on me. You all saw it. He drew on me!"

Nobody spoke. Mr. McGee backed toward the door, still holding his gun. He stepped through and disappeared.

The men who had been with Jenkins knelt at his side. Jenkins wasn't dead, but he was dying. In a weak and barely audible voice, he asked. "Did I get the yellow-bellied sonofabitch? Did I get him?"

A man said, "You got him, Sid. You got him right enough."

That was a lie, but probably justified in view of the fact that Sid was dying. I just stood there, stunned, unable to move. This was a different kind of killing from the one back in Illinois. Those men had been thieves. This one was guilty of nothing but having been with Mr. McGee in the war.

The man on the floor stared up at the faces of those bending over him. He whispered, "It's true. He panicked and ran off and left half his company."

I heard myself asking, "Would it have been any different if he'd stayed?"

"You're damned right it would. The whole company could've made an orderly retreat. Sure, we'd have lost some men. But not half the company."

The man bending over Sid had glanced up when I spoke. Now he was staring at me as if I was the one who had shot his friend instead of Mr. McGee. I knew I had better get out of there while I could. Besides, I'd found out what I wanted to know, and I sure couldn't help anybody by staying.

His face twisting, Sid said, "God it hurts! Oh, God!"

The other man returned his attention to his friend on the floor. I pushed through the crowd toward the door, my hand resting on my gun. I didn't want to hurt anybody but I sure didn't intend to let them kill me for something Mr. McGee had done.

I reached the door and stepped out into the crisp night air. Mr. McGee was gone. Slowly I walked in the direction of our camp.

I figured that now I understood what made Mr. McGee the way he was. He had panicked and fled from the ambush into which he'd led his company. He had branded himself a coward even if the Army hadn't branded him. Now he was dedicating his life to proving that he was not a coward, that, in fact, he had more courage than most.

It explained why he had made my troubles his, facing the thieves who had stolen my mule and gun, risking his life doing so. It explained his preoccupation with gunplay and his eagerness to get into every fight.

I walked slowly back to our camp at the edge of the settlement. Mr. McGee had built a small fire. He was hunkered at the side of it, staring morosely into the flames.

He glanced up at me, then quickly glanced away again. I didn't say anything because I knew he'd twist anything I said.

The silence dragged on until it was extremely uncomfortable. Finally he said, "He's a liar!"

I couldn't resist saying, "Was."

"All right. He's dead. The sonofabitch deserved to die for calling me a coward in front of all those men."

I said, "He believed it, even if it wasn't true."

"Well, he was wrong! It wasn't true! We fought our way out of that ambush. I saved half the company, even if I couldn't save it all. None of the men I saved said what he did. By God, you can bet on that!"

I went over to the fire. In that moment I felt older than Mr. McGee. I said. "You don't have to convince me. It's none of my business. Besides, it's over and done with. It happened a long time ago."

"Well, I don't like somebody coming around and saying something like that about me."

I had to say it because it needed to be said. "Next time, bust the man in the mouth instead of shooting him."

"There won't be any next time."

We hadn't eaten and we didn't even have a coffee pot. I was out of sorts and didn't want to argue any more. On top of that, I didn't like the way I became more and more obligated to Mr. McGee as time went on. Tomorrow, we'd go into Julesburg Station and outfit ourselves. Mr. McGee would pay for it and I'd feel even more obligated to him. But I didn't see any way out of it, unless I was willing to give up the pursuit of Barney and his friends.

We had no blankets. I walked out into the darkness and, mostly by groping and feeling, gathered a big armload of firewood. I carried it back and dumped it beside the fire. Mr. McGee still hunkered there, staring morosely into the flames.

I lay down and closed my eyes, but I could feel Mr. McGee staring at me. It made me uneasy. He'd challenged me once when he was drunk. I had a feeling it was even more certain now that he'd challenge me again. I knew about his failure during the war, and every time he looked at me I'd remind him of that fact even if I never mentioned it again.

The truth was, and I knew it now even if I hadn't known it earlier, that any man can fail. Nobody reacts with intrepid courage in every situation he faces all through his life. Nobody is perfect, but Mr. McGee seemed to demand perfection of himself, and because he couldn't deliver it he always felt guilty and had to keep proving himself, time and time again.

I finally went to sleep. I awoke a couple of times during the night. The first time, Mr. McGee was still staring into the fire. The second, he was lying beside it, apparently asleep.

Near dawn, too cold to sleep any more, I got up and rebuilt the fire. I crouched over it until the sky turned gray, trying to get warm.

Mr. McGee got up, eyes red from lack of sleep, his face morose. Because I didn't particularly want to talk to him, I went to where the horses were, untied and led them back to the fire.

Glumly we mounted and rode toward the settlement. The sun came up. We had to wait half an hour for the general store to open up. When it did, Mr. McGee bought saddles, saddle blankets, bridles, and blankets. He bought a sack of food and a couple of canteens. He paid for all these things with gold he took out of a money belt he had strapped around his waist. Faults he might have. Stinginess wasn't one of them.

He'd have been more comfortable going on without me, and I couldn't understand why he did not. I made up my mind that I wasn't going to be critical of him, no matter what. He had his faults like anybody did, but he'd been a good friend to me. We went to the livery and traded horses, then got breakfast at a tiny sod restaurant run by a middle-aged man and his wife. Finished, we mounted and rode west along the Platte.

A mile or so out of town we both dismounted to study the tracks in the dusty road. Walking, occasionally kneeling, we finally picked out the tracks left by the horses of Barney and the two with him.

I was greatly relieved to have a trail again. Fleeing from the Indians, I'd been afraid we'd never pick it up again.

Strangely enough, finding it seemed to give me no real pleasure. My enthusiasm for the chase and for the vengeance that lay at the end of it had been declining steadily over the past few weeks.

12

Tracking is mostly a matter of experience, of learning what to look for, and learning the things that made a track deteriorate and thus reveal its age. For weeks now, Mr. McGee and I had been following trail. Through experience I had become, if not exactly expert, pretty good at it.

Trailing Barney and his friends was not difficult. In most places the road was soft enough for their horses' tracks to plainly show. But, about a dozen miles west of Julesburg, they suddenly left the road and headed for the river.

It is also simple, by reading trail, to judge the speed at which the quarry is traveling. Leaving the road, all three of the fugitives were galloping.

Curiously, Mr. McGee and I followed them. They had ridden at a hard gallop almost to the river. About fifteen or twenty yards short of it, other tracks appeared, overlaid by those of the three men we were following. They were moccasin tracks, small and plainly the tracks of women, two of them. Still short of the river, Barney and those with him had left their running horses and had caught the Indian women and wrestled them to the ground.

Reading the scuffed marks in the soft ground, I felt my face getting hot, felt fury rising inside of me. I had nearly succeeded in putting the images of my dead parents out of my thoughts and mind. These tracks suddenly brought them back, particularly the memory of my mother lying dead and naked in the house. The three men must have spotted two Indian women from the road. They had caught and raped them here. I raised my glance and studied the surrounding area.

I saw no bodies, which puzzled me. Mr. McGee was staring at me but I avoided his glance. I straightened and made a circle of the area. It was only a moment before I found what I was looking for, the clear imprints in the sand of one body, the running footprints of the other woman trying to escape.

Surrounding the imprint left in the dry sand by the body of the Indian woman were many other footprints, also moccasin prints, but larger. These were the prints of the Indian men, who had arrived on the scene too late to save one of the women, barely in time to save the life of the second one.

Once more I raised my head and stared around. Something caught my eye at the edge of the cottonwoods that lined the river bank. I knew what it was even before I reached it.

It was the naked, bloodstained body of a man, a white man. I recognized him instantly as one of those who had attacked and killed my folks. It was the dark-haired, bearded one.

His skull was crushed, apparently by the blow of a gun barrel or war club. That blow must have killed him instantly. But such a quick death had been far from satisfying to the Indians.

They had stripped him, slashing his clothes in their haste. They had mutilated him in a particularly meaningful way, considering what he had done. My stomach cramped and I turned away.

Mr. McGee was still watching me. I walked angrily away from him and began another, larger circle of the entire area. Halfway around it I picked up the tracks of two shod horses, running hard, and overlying them the unshod tracks of a dozen Indian ponies. Turning, I went back to Mr. McGee. "They left with a dozen Indians after them. Some of the Indians must have stayed behind to take care of that." I gestured toward the dead man.

Mr. McGee had already mounted his horse. He said, "One down and two to go."

I didn't answer him. I mounted and took the trail, kicking my horse into a steady trot.

I told myself angrily that I ought to feel satisfied. One of the men I had sworn to kill was dead. Maybe his death hadn't been as slow or as painful as I'd have liked, but he had known it was coming and he must have been thoroughly terrified. He had been caught in a brutal and criminal act and this time had paid for his crime.

But I didn't feel satisfied. I only felt sickened and numb. Was I going to feel the same way when I finally caught up with the other two?

Mr. McGee rode about ten yards behind. With some wonder I realized that the change of roles was finally complete. I was doing the tracking now. I was riding in the lead. The trouble was, I didn't like the role I had unintentionally assumed.

Mr. McGee hadn't mentioned burying the dead man and neither had I. I didn't figure he was entitled to a Christian burial. Not a criminal like him. And certainly not by me. Let the buzzards tear him apart or let him rot in the sun.

It was almost immediatey apparent to me that neither the two remaining whites nor the pursuing Indians could long maintain the pace at which they had been traveling, and I was right. About two miles from the place the Indians had surprised the three, I came to a lot of scuffed tracks and torn-up ground. A dead horse lay here, one of those that had belonged to the whites. Bridle, saddle, and saddle blanket had been stripped from him but I could tell him by the iron shoes on his feet.

I halted and dismounted. I had earlier decided that all these tracks had been made yesterday afternoon, so there was no particular urgency about our following.

Mr. McGee now dismounted too and wandered around, studying the ground. Finally he said, "I make it about a dozen Indians. That the way you come out?"

"About."

"They caught our friends and carried them away. Find any blood?"

"Only near the horse."

"Then they're both probably alive. Or were yesterday."

"What do you figure the Indians would do with them?"

"After what they did to those two Indian women? They'll kill 'em, but likely not right away, if what I've heard is true. They'll let them sweat for a day or two. Then they'll stake 'em out and let the women work on them. If those two are lucky, they'll die in six or eight hours. If they're not lucky, it might take days, with them conscious every minute of the time."

I said, "I've got to know."

"Sure you do."

"Then we'll follow them."

"Just so we don't get ourselves caught. In the mood they're in right now, those Indians will give the same treatment to any white man they catch."

"We'll be careful." I mounted my horse, picked up the trail of the Indian ponies, and followed it.

They now were traveling at a more leisurely pace. We'd found no sign of an Indian village, so I had to assume this group had been traveling, perhaps from one village to another, maybe scouting for buffalo. Why women had been traveling with them, or why they had left the Indian women alone, even for a short time, I couldn't guess. I knew practically nothing about Indians, so this particular circumstance didn't even strike me as being strange.

The day dragged past. The trail left the river and headed in a northwesterly direction. We found the place they had camped, and I took fifteen or twenty minutes to study the ground. I found where the two captives had lain all night, but I found nothing to indicate they had been tortured or otherwide abused. Mr. McGee said, "Letting them sweat."

I could imagine the captives' state of mind. They knew damned well they were going to be tortured and ultimately killed. Like everybody back East, they had heard plenty of tales about how the Indians treated captives, particularly those they had cause to hate. They knew death would be long in coming and sweetly welcome when it did. They were sweating; they were suffering. I knew I ought to feel a lot more satisfaction than I did.

I suppose the truth was that I wanted the men dead. No more and no less than that. I wanted this quest for vengeance to be finished. I wanted to turn to something else. Maybe when we'd left Illinois I'd had nothing else in mind. But a lot of time had passed since then. A lot of things had happened. I had changed and I had matured. I was tired of traveling with Mr. McGee, tired of the tension that was between us all the time. I wanted to stop traveling. I wanted to find a job of some kind or another and start living like other people did.

I alternated our pace between a lope and trot, taking care that the horses did not become overheated or overly tired. By nightfall, I figured we had gained at least three hours on the Indians. By tomorrow night, I guessed, we might catch up with them, sooner if they reached their village before that time.

It was nearly dark when we stopped. I said, "We'd better make this a cold camp."

Mr. McGee agreed. We staked our horses out where there was grass, ate a little cold food ourselves, and settled down for the night, reasonably sure we would not be discovered by any Indians. If they were like everybody else, they didn't travel during the night.

We wrapped ourselves in our blankets and settled down to sleep. Suddenly, with no warning, Mr. McGee said, "Back there in Julesburg . . . did Sid say anything before he died?"

I didn't answer, because I didn't want to talk about it. Mr. McGee insisted, "Well, did he?"

I said, "Only what he said while you were there."

"And that was what?"

"That you were captain of his company during the war. That you led them into an ambush and then took half the company and left the other half behind."

"You believe the lying sonofabitch?"

I said, "It don't matter what I believe. It's none of my business. It happened a long time ago and it's over."

"But you think it's true." He was stubbornly insistent.

Irritably I said, "I don't know whether it's true or not. He said it was and you say it's not. What I believe is that both of you believed what you said was true. I can see how he'd think what he did. I can see why you'd do what you did." My irritation was rising as I went on, "What I don't understand is why you had to kill the man for saying what he believed. There's got to be a better way of settling things."

"And what would that be?" he asked sarcastically. "What would you do if somebody called you a stinking coward in front of that many men?"

I shouldn't have said it but I did. "If I wasn't a coward, then somebody calling me one shouldn't bother me too much."

"Are you saying he was right? Are you calling me a coward too?"

Disgustedly I said, "Oh, for God's sake! I'm not saying anything!"

"The hell you're not! I should have killed you that night I took you on."

Once more I should have kept my mouth shut, but I was too disgusted to do what I should. I said, "If you'd kept trying, you'd have been six feet underground."

"Maybe I ought to take you on right now."

The temptation to say, "All right, go ahead," was almost irresistible. I made myself remember all Mr. McGee had done for me. I clenched my fists until I'd gotten myself under control again. Finally I said, "Let's catch up with these Indians first. After that, if you want to have it out, then it's all right with me."

I couldn't see his eyes, and I don't know what mine showed. What I felt was mostly disgust. Fighting just to decide who was best was silly as far as I was concerned. But no matter how I felt, sooner or later I was going to have to fight Mr. McGee—to prove that and only that.

13

I awakened during the night to the chill of a cold, fierce wind blowing hard out of the north. I suppose I had known that winter would eventually catch up with us, but I'd hoped it wouldn't come so soon, because an early snow might mean loss of the trail. It might mean the fugitives would get away.

I lay there shivering until gray began to outline the horizon in the east. Then I got up. I kept the blanket wrapped around my shoulders for warmth as I walked away from camp, looking for dry buffalo chips for fuel.

We were ill equipped to face a winter storm. Neither of us had a coat. All we had were our blankets.

I brought an armload of buffalo chips back to camp and, shielding it with my blanket, kindled a fire. Mr. McGee got up and crouched over it, trying to get warm.

Overhead, low, dark clouds scudded along on the rising wind. I felt a drop of rain, another, and another still. Then, very suddenly, the whole sky was filled with driving granules of sleet.

I went after the horses immediately and led them back to camp. I saddled mine, and Mr. McGee, leaving the fire reluctantly, saddled his. He muttered something about the cold, spread his hands once more to the fire's warmth, then unwillingly mounted his horse.

By now it was light enough to see the ground. I picked up the trail and followed it. Northwesterly it went, mostly straight except when a bluff or dry wash forced a temporary deviation. Apparently the group of Indians knew exactly where they were going, probably to a much larger village.

The sleet changed to snow and the snow thickened, driving now horizontally on the wind. It began to cover the ground and I knew sooner or later I was going to lose the trail, this time probably for good.

Guiltily I realized that a part of me was relieved. I admitted to myself that I didn't really care. I was tired of tracking, tired of nurturing hatred and thirst for revenge.

I thought about my father and wondered what he would say about the way I felt. The hell of it was, I didn't know. I could imagine him being angry because I did not really want to go on. I could also imagine him saying I should stop, that vengeance belonged to the Lord.

Mr. McGee was morose and silent as we rode. He stayed well behind but I seemed to feel the weight of his steady stare on my back. A couple of times I looked around. Neither time was he watching me. Either he was quickly looking away when he saw my head begin to turn, or I was imagining things.

By the time an hour had passed, the ground was covered with half an inch of snow. I could no longer see the prints of the Indians horses' hooves except in a few places where the wind had scoured the ground. But I could still see the deep furrows made by the travois poles.

The snow continued to thicken until it seemed as if we were riding in a void. No longer could I see the ground. Looking back, all I could see of Mr. McGee and his horse was a blurred spot of black. I halted long enough to let him catch up and then went on.

The trail was lost and so was the direction we wanted to go. I had heard stories of people wandering in circles during a blizzard until they became hopelessly confused and lost. I stopped my horse again. When Mr. McGee came abreast I shouted, "How are we going to keep going straight?"

"Use the wind," he shouted back.

"What if it changes?"

"Likely won't! Not today anyhow!"

I wondered why I hadn't thought of that. Keeping the wind on the right quarter, I rode on, thoroughly chilled and beginning to get wet from the melting snow. The whole front of my face was crusted. My hands were numb.

I kept trying to see the ground. Occasionally I would when the snow thinned momentarily. Once I thought I saw the furrows made by the travois poles, but I could not be sure.

Suddenly, immediately ahead of me, a huge, black form materialized. I started violently and grabbed at my gun. The grip was covered with snow and my hand slipped off.

My horse snorted and shied. Mr. McGee, coming up behind, nearly ran into me. More dark figures appeared, saw us, stopped, and then turned and disappeared into the driving snow.

It was the first time in my life I had seen buffalo up close. I had never realized how huge they were. I looked at Mr. McGee. "What should we do?"

"Keep going. I'd guess that the only time they're dangerous is when they stampede. Not much chance of them doing that today."

I kicked my horse in the ribs and he moved ahead. We were now right in the midst of the buffalo. A few of them spooked nervously away but most paid no attention to us other than to raise their shaggy heads and stare.

I knew the trail of the Indians was lost for good. Maybe when the storm was over we'd pick it up again. Maybe not. In any case, there was nothing I could do about it now.

We rode through the scattered buffalo for nearly an hour. Finally they thinned, and at last disappeared. Not long after that, I heard a muffled shout.

I stopped again and Mr. McGee caught up. I said, "Hear that?"

"Uh-huh. Sounded like a white man to me."

I listened intently for the shout to be repeated, wondering how he could tell a white man's shout from that of an Indian. The shout came again. This time the words were distinguishable as English words.

I kicked my horse's ribs. Immediately ahead, I saw the towering shape of a cottonwood. A few moments later a wagon materialized, and a little after that, a group of horses, corraled by rope stretched between four cottonwoods. A man yelled, "Hey! Who the hell are you?"

I dismounted. A big, shaggy man came toward me. I could smell both him and the camp. The stench was overpowering. It was the smell of decaying flesh, of drying hides, of smoke, of half a dozen other, indistinguishable things. The man boomed, "Well, I'll be damned. It's a kid." He looked beyond me at Mr. McGee. "Where the hell are you two goin' in this storm?"

I didn't answer him and neither did Mr. McGee. Both of us were looking at the huge fire the group had going in the middle of their camp. We tied our horses to the rear wheel of the wagon and walked to it, the man following.

I guessed, from the smell, that these men were hunting buffalo. I got as close to the fire as I could. In spite of the heat I began to shiver violently. I kept turning myself like a piece of meat on a spit. The crusted snow on my face and clothes thawed and disappeared, and my clothes began to steam.

The man had followed us to the fire. My hands were hurting now as they got warm. The man repeated, "What the hell are you two doing away out here?"

I said, "Tracking some Indians. You seen anything of them?"

"Ain't seen 'em. One of the boys cut their trail, though, early this morning. North of here. Why you trailin' 'em?"

"They've got two white men prisoners."

"Friends of yours?"

"Not exactly."

"What do you mean by that?"

I'd rather have dropped it, but he didn't seem to want me to. I said, "We were trailing three white men. They caught a couple of Indian squaws and killed one of them. The Indians caught them and killed one of them. They took the others prisoner."

"I sure don't envy them two," the man breathed. "I sure as hell don't." He was silent a moment. Then he stuck out a calloused and incredibly dirty hand. "I'm Ben Harris."

I said, "Jason Willard. This is Mr. McGee."

The man shook my hand, then shook Mr. McGee's. He studied Mr. McGee's face closely a moment, then studied mine. When he spoke again, it was not to Mr. McGee, the older, but to me, the younger. "Why was you followin' 'em?"

I was getting warm and drowsy. I'd wanted to drop the conversation but I was glad for the fire and I knew in a little bit we'd get coffee and something to eat. In return, the least I could do was be sociable. I said, "They killed my folks back in Illinois."

"And you followed 'em this far?" His voice was incredulous.

I said, "We didn't trail them all the way."

Three other men had by now joined us at the fire. Ben Harris said, "This here is Hughie Marks. And Dan Ericson. And Julius Isaacs. Marks and Isaacs are skinners. Ericson's a hunter."

The men shook hands with Mr. McGee and me. I saw a woman on the other side of the fire. She was Indian, dressed in a long deerskin dress and moccasins. A blanket was wrapped around her shoulders for warmth. She raked some coals out of the fire with a stick, shoved some rocks into place, and put on an iron pot to cook. She also had a blackened coffee pot, and she arranged it over the fire similarly. Finished, she glanced up, and for an instant her glance met mine.

She was young. She didn't look much older than I

was. Her glance fell away. She got up and disappeared silently into the driving snow.

I switched my glance back to the buffalo hunters. All of them were bearded; all had long, uncut hair. Their clothes were caked with dry blood and tallow. I edged around so that I'd be upwind from them. Ben Harris gave me a toothy grin that had no humor in it. "Smell too much fer you?"

I didn't know what to say. I didn't want to insult the man, because Mr. McGee and I needed shelter and warmth and food. I grinned at Harris. "You got to admit it's a little strong."

His grin widened. Now it had genuine warmth to it. "I guess you're right. Man gets used to it and forgets it's there."

I didn't see how anybody could get used to a stench like that. Not when every once in a while your nose would catch a breath of the clean, pure air blowing in on the wind.

Harris said, "We'll have somethin' to eat before long. You boys will stay, won't you?"

I glanced at Mr. McGee. His eyes were fixed on the spot where the Indian girl had disappeared from sight. I said, "Sure we'll stay."

I don't know why I suddenly felt so uneasy. Maybe it was the look on Mr. McGee's face as he stared after the Indian girl.

But I was dry now, and warm. I felt like going to sleep. I knew we'd go on following the Indians after the weather cleared, but I could summon up no real enthusiasm for it.

Harris left and came back with a brown bottle half filled with whiskey. He offered it to me, but I turned him down. Grinning, he offered the bottle to Mr. McGee, who took a long drink and afterward shuddered and made a face. Harris laughed uproariously.

Mr. McGee took another drink, managing this one without either the grimace or the shudder. My uneasiness increased as I noticed that Mr. McGee kept looking around the buffalo hunters' camp.

I knew what was on his mind. The Indian girl. And I had a premonition that trouble, bad trouble, was going to break out before we left this camp.

I felt sorry for the Indian girl. Her face had been pretty, her eyes filled with fright. It had been as if she was begging me for help.

I didn't know if she was a captive or if she was with these men of her own free will. I doubted if she was a captive, because if she had been some measures would have been taken to keep her from running away. On the other hand, if she was free to go any time she wished, why had her eyes begged me silently for help?

She came back and stirred the pot. She moved the coffee pot back from the fire a little way. Harris said, "Coffee's ready. You boys want a cup?"

Both Mr. McGee and I said we did. Harris got a couple of tin cups and filled them for us.

Mr. McGee sipped his, but over the rim of the cup, his eyes continued to search the curtain of driving snow. I suddenly knew that we'd be smart if we rode away now, snow or no snow. I knew I was going to be sorry if we did not.

But I said nothing and I didn't move, because it would do no good. Mr. McGee wouldn't leave and I couldn't force him to do anything.

Harris boomed, "Hughie, put them two horses in the corral. Mr. Willard an' Mr. McGee are stayin' the night with us."

Hughie left the fire and headed for the wagon where our horses had been tied. I drank my coffee, feeling the welcome warmth in my stomach. But I couldn't get rid of the coldness in my chest. I wished we'd never happened on this camp.

14

After a while, when the food was done, the Indian girl came and lifted the pot off the fire. She tasted the meat, seemed satisfied, and set the pot aside. Harris told Mr. McGee and me to help ourselves and we did. I knew the meat was buffalo, and I expected it to be tough, but it wasn't. It was tender and juicy and the best thing I'd had to eat for weeks. I had another cup of coffee to go with it.

As soon as we were through with our plates, the Indian girl took them and cleaned them, and two of the buffalo hunters, who had been waiting for them, took them and began to eat. The snow hadn't let up. There was about four inches on the ground away from the fire where the warmth didn't melt it as quickly as it fell.

The hunters had made shelter for themselves by stretching buffalo hides between the trees. Harris said, "You two can sleep under the wagon if you're a mind."

I thanked him and got my blanket from behind my saddle. I walked over to the wagon and crawled underneath where the ground was dry. I hollowed out a little place for my hip bone and lay down, covering myself. I knew I ought to be worrying about Mr. McGee and that Indian squaw, but I didn't see what good my worrying would do. Nothing was going to stop Mr. McGee, and I had just as well get some rest.

I closed my eyes and was almost immediately asleep. I woke up once, and heard shouting, drunken voices. I listened for a few minutes, then went back to sleep again.

The second time I woke up, there was noise in the wagon over my head. They were struggling sounds and I half raised up. Then I heard Mr. McGee's voice and a little later heard a woman's giggle. From that I knew she was with him of her own free will. Maybe she was trying to get him to take her away from the hunters, and maybe lying with him was the price she figured she had to pay.

I listened, feeling angry, but stirred up too because I knew what was going on. I'd never had a woman myself but this didn't mean I'd never wanted one. The sounds finally stopped. For a long time there was complete silence and I supposed both Mr. McGee and the Indian woman had gone to sleep.

But I couldn't go back to sleep. I was too stirred up. I lay awake for what was probably half an hour. Then I heard a man's voice calling out from the direction of the buffalo hide shelters stretched between the trees. I waited a minute, thinking maybe whoever had called out would go back to sleep. But he didn't. He called out again, and this time his voice sounded wide-awake.

It was plain even to me who he was calling for. The Indian girl. He'd missed her when he awakened and now was wondering where she was.

I threw off the blanket and got up. I reached into the wagon to shake Mr. McGee awake. My hand encountered the softness of the Indian girl's body instead. I whispered urgently, "You'd better get back to your own bed before somebody gets killed. I doubt if she understood any of my words but she sure as hell understood my tone of voice. Maybe she'd also heard Harris' second shout.

She raised up and tried to get out of the wagon. Mr. McGee held onto her. She began to struggle, and when Mr. McGee still wouldn't let her go, a cry escaped her lips.

I thought, "Oh, God!" because I knew Harris couldn't help but hear. Maybe the girl, faced with discovery, was trying to make Harris believe she had been forced, or maybe the cry slipped out of her before she realized it might be heard. Anyway, I heard a bellow from Harris and knew he was coming, bringing trouble along with him.

Over my head there were now violent sounds of struggle inside the wagon. The girl must have bitten Mr. McGee trying to get away from him, because I heard him howl. A moment later the girl dropped from the wagon, clutching her clothes around her.

She should have run straight away into the darkness beyond the camp. That would have given Harris time to simmer down. Instead, she ran straight toward him.

The snow had stopped. The fires had almost completely died, but there was light from the stars and from a crescent moon. The girl's bare skin gleamed in that cold light as she ran toward the place from which Harris' shout had come.

Harris caught her thirty or forty feet from the wagon. There was a violent struggle and some savage curses from Harris. I heard the sounds of his fists striking her, and I heard her whimpering cries of pain.

I turned my head. Mr. McGee was climbing out of the wagon, his pants in his hand. I said angrily, "You'd better get over there and take your share of the blame, hadn't you? What did you promise her, anyway? To take her back to the Indians?"

He swung a hand involuntarily and it struck me squarely in the mouth. I could taste blood and I was suddenly more furiously angry than I had ever been before in my life. I might have returned the blow, but I got no chance. The Indian girl screamed. The scream almost instantly died to moans that were worse than the scream had been.

I knew Harris had hurt her bad. I snatched up my gun belt and ran, buckling it on as I did. Mr. McGee came along close behind, carrying his pants.

The girl lay motionless in the snow. Stars and cresent moon didn't provide much light, but there was enough to see her nearly naked body, to see the scarlet of her blood staining the whiteness of the snow and the handle of the knife protruding from her breast.

I stopped, stunned and numb. It had happened with such a terrible suddenness that for a moment I was hardly able to think.

Then my anger began to grow, dwarfing the fury I had felt a few moments before when Mr. McGee struck me on the mouth.

Behind Harris, the other hunters were coming, barefooted in the snow, most clutching either blankets or clothes around them against the cold. I heard my own voice saying, "You didn't have to kill her. By God, you didn't have to do that!"

Standing over her, legs spread, he faced me. I couldn't see his expression but I could imagine what it was. He said in a tight, angry voice, "Was it you?"

I opened my mouth to answer but I didn't get the chance. Behind me Mr. McGee said, "No. It wasn't him. It was me, and I ain't the first she's laid up with. What'd you have to kill her for?"

I said, "Why the hell don't you just shut your mouth?"

The Indian girl had been pretty, probably a captive, getting along and staying alive the best way she could. I had a hunch the only reason she'd taken up with Mr. McGee was in hopes he'd rescue her. To hear her talked about now as if she was a slut made me furious.

Harris was silent, dangerously so, I realized. Suddenly he leaned down and snatched the knife out of the Indian girl. With a roar like a bull, he charged at me. No. Not at me. He was after Mr. McGee and I happened to be in the way.

Mr. McGee didn't have a weapon. He didn't even have on his pants. Last I'd seen he had been holding them in his hand. If I let Harris get past me, Mr. McGee was dead.

The lightning thought crossed my mind, Why not? and then I knew why not. Mr. McGee had done too much for me to let him die here in the snow at the hands of a crazed squaw man. I yelled, "Harris! Stop where you are or I'll shoot!" I didn't even have my gun in my hand, but belt and holstered gun were around my waist.

Harris didn't stop and there sure wasn't time for any more talk. It was fish or cut bait, and I fished. I yanked my gun out of its holster so fast I surprised even myself. As it came up my thumb was pulling the hammer back. I fired the instant the gun came level, into Harris who by then was less than a foot away. I knew the bullet struck him squarely in the chest and I knew he was dead, but I knew his knife could hurt me just the same.

I jumped to one side and he went by. The knife grazed my forearm, bringing a rush of blood. He collapsed just beyond me at Mr. McGee's feet.

At the other hunters, I yelled, "He's dead! Stay where you are and maybe the rest of you will stay alive!"

They stopped. I didn't even turn my head and look at Mr. McGee. I said disgustedly, "Get your goddam pants on and get the horses while I hold them here."

He didn't say anything but I knew he had done what I told him to. I stood there holding a gun on these hunters, thinking they had welcomed us and fed us and given us shelter for the night. In return, Mr. McGee had stolen Harris' squaw, getting her killed in the bargain, and now I'd had to kill Harris to keep him from killing Mr. McGee. The whole thing sickened me.

It seemed like a long time before Mr. McGee appeared beside me holding our horses' reins. I said, "My hat and blanket are under the wagon. Get them." I didn't even try to make it a request. It was an order, one he instantly obeyed. I handed him the gun, while I draped the blanket around my shoulders and crammed my hat down on my head. Then I took it back. I didn't have to worry about the hunters anymore. None of them were armed, and by the time they got to their guns, we'd be gone.

I holstered my gun, mounted, and rode away into the

night. I heard the hooves of Mr. McGee's horse following. I maintained a steady trot, not looking back.

Behind us there was some shouting, a buffalo gun boomed out a couple of times, but the bullets came noplace near to us.

I kept thinking about the Indian girl. I couldn't get her face out of my thoughts, and I couldn't forget the sight of her leaving the wagon with something clutched around her that didn't even begin to hide her nakedness. I remembered the way she had felt when my hand encountered her instead of Mr. McGee when I reached into the wagon to wake him up.

We rode in silence for a couple or three hours. Finally the sky in the east grayed and then began to turn pink.

The country was covered with a blanket of snow. It was white as far as I could see. Bluffs and trees and gulches showed up black, but otherwise everything was white.

I hadn't spoken to Mr. McGee since leaving the hunters' camp. To tell the truth, I didn't care if I ever spoke to him again. As the sun came up, he called out from behind, "No call to stay mad all day. She was only a goddam Indian squaw."

I stopped my horse and swung around. I had no idea what my face looked like, but if it looked as furious as I felt inside it wasn't any wonder that Mr. McGee looked scared. I said, "You sonofabitch! She was good enough to go to bed with. She was good enough to feed us. But not good enough, by God, to feel sorry about now that she's dead!"

He held his hand out, palm forward, as if to placate me. He said. "Whoa now, Jason. I didn't mean no harm. But hell, everybody knows Indians ain't like us."

I said contemptuously, "Damn you to hell, you got me to kill for you again."

"Yeah, an' you saved my life. I won't forget it, Jason. I surely won't."

I said, "It's the last time. Maybe I owed you something once, but I've paid off. We're square. I don't owe you a goddam thing anymore."

"All right. All right. You don't owe me a thing. Does that mean we can't be friends?"

"I don't want to be friends with you. You use me and I don't like being used. You just figure out which way you want to go and I'll go the other way."

"What about the two that killed your folks? You going to give up hunting them?"

"Maybe. I don't know." I really didn't know. Killing sickened me and I knew when I caught up there'd be more killing.

"You ain't telling me we came all this way just to give up?"

"Maybe I'll go on."

"Then let me go with you. I won't give you no more trouble, Jason. I promise you."

It suddenly struck me how strange this was. Here we sat, hundreds of miles from anything, in the middle of thousands of square miles of empty, snow-covered prairie. Neither of us even had a coat. And we were arguing.

Finally I shrugged, mostly because I didn't want to argue anymore. I said, "All right. But no more trouble and no more fights."

"I swear it. No more trouble and no more fights."

I couldn't resist what I said next. "You don't have to prove how big a man you are every day. What happened to you during the war is over with."

I knew the minute the words were out that I should have kept my big mouth shut. Mr. McGee's eyes glittered and he quickly looked down at the ground. But he didn't look down quickly enough to hide that look from me.

I'd said he could come along with me and I'd stick by what I'd said. But I was already sorry for it.

Mr. McGee was dangerous. Death would follow him no matter where he went. If he was with me, I might be the instrument of death.

15

The sun melted most of the snow before noon, leaving the land muddy and soft underfoot. I had no hope we'd pick up the Indians' trail, and I'd gotten to where I didn't really care anymore. I went on because I didn't know what else to do and because chasing the men who had killed my folks gave me something to do. But my heart wasn't in it, and I'd lived with my folks long enough to know that if I could have asked them they'd respect my decision no matter what it was.

It was late October and the sun got plenty hot in the middle of the day in spite of the chill the snow had put into the air. Some places, where there wasn't any grass, the land actually steamed.

In mid-afternoon, we sighted a herd of buffalo ahead of us. I stopped on a little ridge and stared in amazement at them. I hadn't believed it possible for a herd of wild animals to be this huge. They blackened the land from the horizon on our right to the horizon on our left, and all the way to the horizon straight ahead. They weren't packed solid, of course, but they were close enough together so that there weren't many places you could see the ground, at least from this far away.

Mr. McGee pulled his horse to a halt at my side. He said, "There's our supper, Jason."

I nodded. Getting one of the huge beasts would be easy enough. But for a while I sat there in awe, staring at the slowly moving herd. They were headed south, probably started in that direction by last night's storm. I said, "That meat we had last night was good. What part of the critter did it come from?"

"The hump. It's all the hunters eat."

It seemed like an awful waste to me, but from a practical standpoint there was no way on earth the huge carcasses could be utilized. By the time they could be transported to a town or settlement, the meat would be spoiled. Only the Indians could make use of all the buffalo, and only because they lived here where the buffalo were.

The near edge of the migrating herd was still five or six miles away. I touched my horse's sides with my heels and rode on. Once more Mr. McGee seemed content to fall in behind. For some reason I looked back at his face.

He was watching me intently. I can't say exactly what was in his expression, but it wasn't pleasant to have a man who looked at me like that riding behind. I doubted if he'd shoot me, but I had seen the unmistakable desire to do so in his eyes. Sometime, and soon, we would have to fight it out. He wouldn't leave me and he wouldn't let me leave him. Unless one of us was killed accidentally or by someone else, our meeting was inevitable.

I considered it and I realized I was going to be glad when Mr. McGee was dead. I might have already become the leader but I wasn't free. He still dominated me, even though he pretended to follow me. As long as he was with me I would go on doing what he wanted me to do.

We finally reached the edge of the herd and stopped a couple or three hundred yards away. The buffalo didn't pay any attention to us, perhaps feeling security in the enormity of the herd. I rode up a little brushy draw and got off my horse. I crawled to the lip of the draw and waited for one of the buffalo to come within pistol range.

I didn't have long to wait. A young bull passed within about thirty feet. I drew a careful bead on his neck, just behind his head, and fired.

He went down like he'd been clubbed. He kicked a couple of times and then lay still.

Those behind him, downwind, stopped, bunching as more animals crowded them from the rear. They smelled the blood and began to snort and paw the ground. I got my horse, mounted, and rode up out of the draw. Mr. McGee followed me. I asked, "You think they'd charge?"

He shook his head, but I stayed ready in case they did. He was right, though. After a while the pressure behind them became too great and they moved on, swerving to give us room.

Mr. McGee borrowed my knife. He skinned the hump and then cut off a huge chunk of meat. We went back into the draw from which I'd shot the buffalo. It didn't occur to me that it might be dangerous camping here. I thought since we were on the edge of the herd that we'd be all right.

We gathered wood and built a fire. Mr. McGee was grumbling about having left his gun behind at the buffalo hunters' camp. We broiled the meat on sticks. It wasn't near as tender as what we'd had at the hunters' camp last night but it was good. After we'd eaten, I found some snow that hadn't melted in the shade of a big rock. I'd left our blackened coffee pot behind, so we had to content ourselves with eating snow. As soon as it got dark, we lay down to sleep. For a while, Mr. McGee stayed up, looking back the way we'd come. I guess he thought the buffalo hunters might be coming after us.

I went to sleep. It was smells that wakened me, the smell of wet hair and the smell of manure. I sat up, and at almost the same time, Mr. McGee sat up too.

We were in this little brushy draw, which was why we hadn't already been trampled by the spreading herd. Now they were on all sides of us. Our horses were stamping their feet nervously and snorting every now and then.

I asked sleepily, "What time is it?"

"Hell, I don't know. What difference does it make?"

"None, I guess. Are they all around us?" It was a silly question. I knew they were. I asked, "What are we going to do?" I was angry with myself for asking him but I always seemed to depend on him in moments of uncertainty or stress.

"Wait until it gets light. We're okay here as long as they keep traveling slow."

"Will they let us ride through them?"

"I don't see why not."

I settled back but I couldn't go to sleep. Those hundreds and thousands of huge hooves made a low rumble in the ground. I lay there listening to it.

The eastern sky finally turned gray. We got up. The air was chill enough so that we could see our breaths. We saddled our horses but kept our blankets around us for warmth.

As usual, I rode out first and Mr. McGee followed me. I came up out of the draw a little uncertainly. Behind me, Mr. McGee said, "Ride with them, but keep angling right."

I followed his instructions. The buffalo to right and left of us shied away, but not even the big bulls offered to fight, probably because we were moving with them and not against the tide. After ten minutes or so I began to relax. Hell, this wasn't going to be so bad. All we had to do was stay alert, but otherwise it looked like everything was going to be all right.

I suddenly realized that my belt and gun were gone. In panic, I stared back in the direction we had come, thinking that in some way I had left them behind. But I hadn't. The belt was strapped around Mr. McGee's waist. I said angrily, "What the hell did you do that for?"

"Your gun? You don't mind me borrowing it for a while, do you?"

"You're damned right I mind! Give it back." I slowed my horse, but Mr. McGee slowed his too. The plodding buffalo pressed against his horse from the rear, bunching up. One big bull bellowed and pawed the ground as if he was going to charge.

Mr. McGee pulled my revolver and shot the bull. The animal went down, front legs folding first, hindquarters folding almost reluctantly. The bull bellowed from the ground, a bloody froth coming from his nose.

I didn't know what to do. I knew it was dangerous for us to stir up these buffalo. We were right in the middle of the biggest herd in the country, probably, and we'd better not do anything stupid if we knew what was good for us. I asked angrily. "What the hell did you do that for?"

"Why not?" He was grinning at me. His eyes were bright, as if he was enjoying himself. Deliberately, he shot another bull. This one went down, wounded but fighting to get up, not twenty feet from the first.

I yelled, "Damn you, stop it! You trying to get both of us killed?"

His grin widened. "Scared, Jason?"

"Damn right I'm scared! You should be too. What if these damn animals stampede?"

Instead of answering, Mr. McGee shot a third, and then a fourth. Deliberately, he reloaded my gun, leaving one cartridge in the cylinder to discourage any ideas I might get of rushing him.

I said, "For Christ's sake, put that damn thing away."

He finished reloading, and deliberately began shooting more buffalo. By now, they had bunched up behind us solid for a couple of hundred yards. Mr. McGee shot four more and began reloading again.

Several bulls were pawing the ground and snorting ferociously. Ahead of us, the herd had cleared out for about a quarter mile. Suddenly, one enormous old bull stopped pawing the ground and charged. Mr. McGee was caught with an empty gun. He had no choice but to flee. I caught a glimpse of his face as he kicked his terrified horse in the ribs. It was white and scared, as much so as mine must have been. In an instant his horse was in full gallop, and mine wasn't far behind.

As if our flight had been some kind of signal, the buffalo behind the charging bull surged into a run and in less time than it takes to tell it, several hundred buffalo were charging after us. I glanced ahead and saw that we were rapidly overtaking the slower moving buffalo ahead of us.

Given open prairie, I supposed we could have escaped the charging animals behind us with little trouble. But with those bunched animals ahead, we had no chance. I bawled, "You goddam fool! Now look what you've done!" Putting blame on him didn't do any good, but it sure made me feel better.

We came up against the massed buffalo ahead of us. Frightened, they too surged into a run, but more buffalo ahead of them prevented them from staying out of our way. In an instant we were caught between the charging buffalo behind and those ahead, jammed in so tight we couldn't move except with the accelerating herd.

I glanced around, looking for some way out. There wasn't any. We were hemmed in on all sides, with no hope of escape. Our only chance was to ride it out, and hope neither of our horses stumbled or fell. The only trouble with riding it out was that gradually the panic Mr. McGee had started was spreading through the surrounding herd. The pace increased until our horses were galloping to keep up.

Ahead of me, Mr. McGee finished reloading my gun for the second time. I hoped he wasn't going to shoot any more buffalo, but I needn't have worried. He'd lost all his taste for that sport by now. He holstered the gun.

I was maybe twenty-five or thirty feet away from him. Between us was a solid wall of shaggy backs, so close-packed it looked like I could dismount and walk on them.

The air was filled with dust clouds, despite the snow that had fallen night before last. I suppose either the body heat of the enormous herd of buffalo had dried the ground, or else that their hooves had pounded through the thin coating of mud on top of the ground to the dust beneath.

Besides the dust there was a choking smell, of hair, animal sweat, and manure. I found it hard to breathe, and under my breath I cursed Mr. McGee more bitterly than I have ever cursed anyone. He'd begun the killing for pure sport and it had excited him so much that he'd kept it up.

It seemed like an enternity that we galloped along with the stampeding buffalo. I wondered how long they'd run. It didn't seem likely that they'd stop very soon, because even if some of them felt like it they'd have had no chance, pushed on by the others as they were.

My horse's neck was lathered and so was his rump. Once, he stumbled and might have gone down but for the pressure of buffalo on all sides of him. Horns raked his rump and shoulders. One drew blood from my right leg.

Before us, over the heads of the animals in front and dimly through the clouds of dust, I suddenly saw trees. I considered trying to leave my horse and pull myself into a tree, and I decided I'd do it if I got a chance. I yelled at Mr. McGee and pointed ahead, and he nodded as if he understood.

The herd swept on. Like a flood of water, it poured down into the river bed, crashing through brush, trampling saplings, turning only for the stoutest of the cottonwoods. Ahead of me, Mr. McGee's horse suddenly went down. Horse and Mr. McGee disappeared under the pounding flood of brown bodies.

If I'd had any sense, I'd just have gone on without him. I guess I didn't have that much sense. I tensed, and when I reached the place where he'd gone down, I hauled back on my horse's reins and made him brace himself against the pressure from the rear.

Mr. McGee had taken shelter behind his horse. He'd been trampled some and was covered with mud and manure, but he was able to stand when I came alongside, and able to grab my stirrup and hang on.

I looked down at his face. It was desperate and scared and I wasn't surprised at that. The thought of dying in mud and manure beneath thousands of hooves is enough to terrify any man.

I didn't know what the hell I was going to do. Mr. McGee couldn't hang onto the stirrup for long. My horse wouldn't go a mile bearing double weight. We'd better do something here in this river bed where there at least were trees to shelter us, or both of us were going to die.

Suddenly, straight ahead, loomed the bare and whitened trunk of an enormous, down and dead cottonwood. The buffalo herd split to go around it. We were also forced to detour it, crammed in even more closely than before, but as if by the design of providence, immediately next to the tree. My horse's side scraped against a protruding root, hard enough so I thought it might have ripped him open. Then we were past, and there was a small, clear space in the lee of the tree.

I reined my horse aside. I rode him close up against the down tree. Mr. McGee let go and collapsed onto the ground. I dismounted and immediately tied the horse.

The next thing I did was take my gun and belt from around Mr. McGee's waist and buckle it around my own. Then, I too sat down and heaved a long, prayerful sigh of relief.

16

All the rest of that day we sat in the lee of the down cottonwood while the buffalo herd streamed past. The buffalo continued to run for several hours, but along toward night they slowed to a trot and finally to a walk. By the time darkness fell, they were grazing, the way they had been when we first spotted them.

I sat sour and silent, with my back to part of the dead cottonwood. A couple of times, Mr. McGee tried to start a conversation, but I refused to answer him. I'd made up my mind that we were going to part company. If we did not, he was going to get me killed, but it wasn't altogether that. I just plain didn't approve of the things he did. Killing buffalo just to see them fall wasn't my idea of fun.

My horse was badly scratched from the buffalo horns, and pretty well worn out, but otherwise he was all right. He stood with his head down, and finally I got up and tied him. There wasn't anything for him to eat here anyway, and while it wasn't likely he'd walk out of this shelter and drift with the buffalo, I didn't intend to take any chances of being left out here afoot.

The next day, the buffalo were still streaming past, but the animals were more scattered now and I figured most of the herd had passed. I wanted to get rid of Mr. McGee, but I couldn't very well leave him out here afoot. I'd have to wait until we came to a ranch or settlement where he could get another horse.

We drank what little water was left in our canteens. We had nothing to eat but I didn't want to take time to kill and cook some buffalo meat. Mr. McGee mounted behind me and we started out, threading our way through the scattered, migrating buffalo. I'd shoved my gun down into my belt in front where Mr. McGee couldn't grab it so easily.

About a mile from the riverbed, we came to the edge of the herd. Mr. McGee said, "We'd better get some meat while we can."

I agreed. "All right. Get down. I'll kill one and cut off the hump. You build a fire while I'm gone."

He slid off the horse without saying a word and began to look for dry buffalo chips to burn. I rode back toward the slowly traveling buffalo. I hid myself in some brush at the edge of the riverbed, and when a young buffalo came close enough, I killed it with my revolver. I skinned out the hump and hacked off a big chunk of meat, the way I'd seen Mr. McGee do. I mounted and carried it back to where Mr. McGee was.

He had a fire going, and I'd brought along some sticks on which to broil the meat. We sat beside the fire while the meat cooked, and for the first time I wondered if Mr. McGee might not steal the horse and leave me afoot. We'd come a long way together but we were near the end of the trail and he must have known it as well as I did.

We ate until we didn't want any more. I had dug a hole in the riverbed last night, and we filled our canteens with the water that seeped up into it. We had food and water and a horse and gun, and should be all right. I mounted and Mr. McGee climbed up behind and we rode out again, still heading northwest the way the Indians had been going last time we saw their trail.

All day we traveled. The sun came up and you wouldn't have believed it had snowed two days before. I'd heard about the Rocky Mountains, but I guessed they were still a long way off.

We camped that night on the open prairie and again we ate buffalo meat broiled over a fire made of dry buffalo chips. That night, I didn't sleep very much. I positioned myself close to the horse, and after Mr. Mc-

Gee had gone to sleep, I wrapped the picket rope around my ankle a couple of times. I figured if Mr. McGee tried to take the horse he'd try to take the picket rope as well.

A couple of times during the night I awoke, but both times it was because the horse had come to the end of the picket rope and it had pulled against my ankle, waking me. Mr. McGee was snoring and I felt ashamed of my suspicions. Even so, I knew I was smart for having them. I was growing up. I was learning that the best way to stay alive is not to trust anyone blindly.

We rode out in bright, warm sunlight, and in mid-afternoon we struck a trail crossing from left to right, going north. It was the trail of three horsemen, plainly white men because two of their horses were shod and the third showed signs of having once been shod. I turned into the trail and followed it. I figured maybe the three were heading for a ranch or settlement where I could get rid of Mr. McGee.

Near sundown, I spotted a building ahead. It was a soddy, that is a building built out of blocks of sod cut from the prairie. Stout poles supported the roof, which was also covered with sod. There were a couple of windows made of oiled hide instead of glass, and a big plank door made of the boards from a wagon bed. Out in front was a small pole corral containing half a dozen horses. Smoke came from a rusty chimney, so I knew someone was there.

McGee slid off and headed for the door, while I watered the horse and put him into the corral. I noticed that behind the soddy was an Indian teepee. As I walked toward the soddy door, I saw an Indian woman looking at me from the teepee flap. I thought, "Oh God, not again." I knew I had to cut loose from Mr. McGee and leave before he started going after this Indian squaw the way he had the other one.

I opened the door. The place was so dark it was a while before I could see anything. But I could smell it the minute I opened the door. The smell was composed of liquor, tobacco smoke, sweat, and wood smoke. A voice yelled, "Shut the goddam door!"

I did. Pretty soon I was able to see. There was a swept dirt floor. On the far side of the room was a long bar made of planks resting on flour barrels. There were two homemade tables, with sections of cottonwood log placed around them for seats.

Seven men were in the room, counting Mr. McGee. He was at the bar and he already had a drink in his hand. He yelled, "Come on, Jason, and have a drink!"

I crossed to the bar. I accepted the drink Mr. McGee shoved at me and drank it in a gulp. I thought for a minute I was going to choke. I couldn't get my breath and my throat was on fire. Mr. McGee was laughing and so was the man behind the bar. I finally managed to breathe again and I looked at the man behind the bar. "I've got a good horse and saddle out there. I need a couple of horses in trade. You got anything?"

He glanced at Mr. McGee and then back at me. He said, "Maybe. Let's go take a look."

He went outside and I followed him. Mr. McGee came along behind. We all walked to the corral.

By comparison with the other horses in the corral, mine was a pretty good animal. In fact, he looked like a racehorse alongside the shaggy ponies in the corral. I was looking at the man from the soddy.

He didn't have a beard, but he hadn't shaved for a couple of weeks. His hair was long and dirty, but his clothes were clean, and from that fact I guessed the Indian squaw was his. I glanced at Mr. McGee. He was staring at the teepee out in back. Glancing that way, I saw the squaw watching us.

She wasn't as young as the other one had been, and she was thicker in the body but she was a pretty woman all the same. I turned my attention back to the man as he said, "I can't give you two horses for one."

I had decided that, horses or no, I was going to

leave Mr. McGee right here. I took a chance and said, "All right then, forget it. I'll keep the horse I've got."

He said, "Whoa now, I didn't say we couldn't work something out. That's a good animal you got there."

I said, "Two for one. Any two you've got, just as long as they're sound."

He pretended to look like I'd beaten him. "All right, youngster, but I get the saddle too."

"Done."

"Just to show I'm a good scout, I'll let you take your pick."

I nodded. I went into the corral and picked the strongest-looking horse, a mousy gray with an ugly hammer head. I looked back at the man. "Two bridles."

"All right."

I put a piece of rope around the gray's neck and led him outside. I looked at Mr. McGee. "Take your pick."

He pulled his glance away from the Indian woman and went into the corral. He finally picked a squat, short-legged bay. By then I had the bridle the man had given me on my horse. I jumped to his back, which wasn't hard because he wasn't very high off the ground.

I looked down at Mr. McGee. "This is where we part company."

He looked startled, like he didn't believe he'd heard me right. "What are you talking about?"

"I'm talking about leaving you. Right here. Right now. I saw the way you were eyeing that Indian squaw."

The man from the soddy was looking back and forth from Mr. McGee to me. When I mentioned the Indian squaw, he glanced at the teepee, then at Mr. McGee and he scowled.

Mr. McGee's face got a little red. "Jason, you can't . . . I haven't even got a gun."

"Buy one."

"How will you live? You haven't got any money."

"I'll manage. Don't worry about me."

"You can't do this! What about all I've done for you? I've saved your neck."

"And I've saved yours. Good-bye, Mr. McGee." I reached out my hand, not wanting to leave him with a lot of bitterness.

He looked at it but he didn't take it. He said. "All right, you ungrateful little sonofabitch! Leave! By God I got along fine without you for a long time and I can get along fine without you again."

I said, "Sure," and turned my horse. I rode away without looking back.

The man from the soddy yelled, "How about a bill of sale?"

I turned my head. "Get it from him." The last I saw of Mr. McGee, he was standing there with his legs spread, hands on hips, looking at me the way a father would look at a naughty boy.

Well, to hell with him. This was the best way no matter how you looked at it. For the first time in weeks I had the feeling that maybe Mr. McGee and I wouldn't end up shooting it out with each other.

I was maybe a quarter mile away when I looked back. The man from the soddy was over in front of the teepee, apparently talking to the squaw. Mr. McGee had disappeared. He'd probably gone back inside, I thought. He was probably busy getting as drunk as he could as fast as he could.

At least, tonight, he wouldn't come staggering out, waking me up and wanting to fight. Maybe he'd make a play for the squaw and maybe he'd get killed for his pains, but at least I wasn't going to be a part of it.

I was glad to be rid of him, and I knew what I'd done was right and the only thing I could have done.

But I somehow felt lonesome all the same. I felt more alone than I've ever felt in my life, before or since.

But I was a grown man and I was going to be alone a lot. I'd just as well start getting used to it.

17

The earth and sky had never seemed so big to me and so empty. Except for a few birds, there didn't seem to be another living thing for miles. Once, as I rode along, I asked myself what I really wanted to do, whether I wanted to go on following the men who had killed my folks or not. I decided that I did, a little surprised to realize that it wasn't so much for revenge as to stop them from doing to other people what they'd done to my family. Men like that go on killing and plundering until somebody stops it by killing them.

Ordinarily, it's the law that stops them, but out here there wasn't any law. Only what a man made himself. I thought a little ruefully that I wasn't a man yet, but I'd better act like one or I'd never get old enough to really call myself a man.

I figured I was south of the Indians' trail, so I angled sharply north. I camped that night alone, and cooked a piece of the buffalo hump over a fire of buffalo chips. I didn't have my saddle, but I'd brought along all the things I'd had tied behind it in a gunny sack. I lay down close to the fire, with my gun in my hand, and went right to sleep. Coyotes woke me once, and a second time an owl cry wakened me. The third time it was dawn.

Still angling north, I traveled all that day. I wondered several times what Mr. McGee would do now. Probably head on west to the mines west of Denver, or go all the way to California. Maybe I'd go there too, after I'd caught up with the men I was following. That is, if I was still alive. I figured there was a two-to-one chance, at least, that one of them would kill me before I got both of them. I was good with a gun, but not good enough to face two hardcases like them and win. Whether I liked admitting it or not, I needed Mr. McGee.

I could pretty well guess what he'd done back at that tiny trading post. He'd gotten himself drunk enough to be reckless. Then he'd gone out and made a play for the trader's squaw. He'd probably been caught, and had either been killed for his pains or had killed the trader first. Then he'd fled, probably along my trail. I glanced behind, studying the land behind me carefully, but I saw no sign of him.

That night, I camped in a brushy riverbed, ate some more of the buffalo hump, which by now had a pretty gamy smell, drank some water, and went to sleep again. That night I didn't wake up until dawn grayed the sky. I took time to cook some more of the meat and then threw what was left away because I couldn't stand the smell of it anymore. I rode out, angling north.

All day, I kept watching my back trail. Once, I thought I saw a spiral of dust, but although I watched the spot for nearly ten minutes, I didn't see it again.

In late afternoon, I finally crossed the Indians' trail. I studied it for a long time and finally found the prints of two shod horses among the others. At the same time, I halted and studied my back trail and, sure enough, I picked out a tiny speck I knew was a horse and man about three miles away.

Well, my horse needed a rest and there wasn't any big hurry now, so I stopped to wait. I was curious about what had happened at the little soddy after I had left.

He caught up with me in about half an hour. He needed a shave badly and his eyes were still bloodshot, his skin kind of grayish sallow. He must have been on a monstrous drunk, I thought, probably feeling sorry for himself because I had ridden away and left him.

He had a gun that I supposed he'd bought from one

of the men at the soddy. He dismounted, came to where I was, and hunkered down. He rolled himself a cigarette with papers and a cloth sack of tobacco. He was shamefaced and wouldn't quite meet my eyes. I said, "What happened?"

"Happened?" He tried to act like he didn't know what I was talking about.

"I mean, did you kill anybody?"

He looked hurt that I would think it of him. I asked, "How come you're following me? I told you I was going on alone."

"I kind of feel responsible for you, Jason boy."

"Don't you 'Jason boy' me, you damn old fraud."

"No offense, boy. No offense." Now his tone was wheedling. "I just happen to be travelin' the same way you are. Ain't no harm in two old friends travelin' together, is there, long as neither of them is goin' out of his way?"

"I asked you a question."

"And what was that?" He was all innocence.

"I asked you if you killed anyone."

"And the answer is no, Jason boy. I swear it to you, I do." He looked me straight and steady in the eye.

"All right," I said grudgingly. "I guess it won't do any harm for us to travel together for a while. But I'm warning you—any trouble and we're parting company."

He looked enormously relieved, though I can't imagine why it was so important to him to get back into my good graces and travel along with me. I mounted my horse and he mounted his. First thing he said was, "First chance we get, we'll buy us saddles and good horses, Jason boy. I won a little money in a poker game back there."

I said irritably. "Don't call me 'Jason boy,' damn it!"

"All right. All right!"

I didn't know whether he'd won some money in a poker game or whether he'd held up the men at the soddy. I didn't know whether to believe anything he said. I'd never actually suspected him of stealing, but by now I was ready to believe anything of him.

Furthermore, I had a sneaking, uneasy feeling I was going to regret letting him come along. But I'd done it in a weak moment and I couldn't go back on my word.

When he reached a place where the ground was soft, Mr. McGee got down and carefully studied the Indians' trail. Looking up, he said, "Day and a half old. Same bunch we were trailing before."

"All right."

"Know what you're going to do when you catch up with them?"

I shook my head. "The best I can, I guess."

"You're going to need me."

"Maybe," I said grudgingly.

We traveled steadily until dark and made a cold camp on the open plain. Neither of us had anything to eat, so we drank some water out of our canteens and lay down to sleep.

I lay awake for a little while, wondering if I was ever going to succeed in getting rid of Mr. McGee, short of killing him. Lately he hadn't shown any signs of wanting to challenge me but I was pretty sure the idea hadn't left his thoughts. Maybe the reason he seemed to have forgotten it was that he no longer thought he had a chance of beating me.

I finally dropped off to sleep and wakened when the first streaks of light showed in the east. I spoke to Mr. McGee and he got up. Once more we drank a little water in lieu of food and took the trail.

It looked to me like the Indians were just poking along. Their horses appeared to be traveling at a walk, and they stopped often, maybe to rest the horses, maybe just to talk. In mid-afternoon I began to get a little spooky about catching up with them unexpectedly. I began leaving the trail whenever there was a ridge ahead, and circling, so that I'd be sure of seeing them before they saw me.

As it turned out, that particular bit of caution wasn't necessary. We heard shooting in the distance, faint popping sounds more like firecrackers than guns. We rode up the side of the next ridge, dismounting before we reached the top and traveling the last fifty feet or so on hands and knees.

About three-quarters of a mile ahead, there were a couple of buildings and a corral. A road running in a southwesterly direction went past the building. Judging from the size of the corral, and from the coach parked beside it, I guessed the building was a stagecoach way station. The Indians seemed to be besieging it, probably after the horses in the corral.

I looked at Mr. McGee. His eyes were bright with the excitement that always showed in them when a fight was imminent. I asked, "What do we do?"

"Why we help 'em, Jason. That's what we do."

"We haven't got much chance of getting through all those Indians. We could wait until it gets dark."

"Them people down there might need our help."

I knew it was no use arguing. Something was driving Mr. McGee, that old charge of cowardice during the war, I guessed, and every time there was the chance of a fight he seemed to think he had to get right into the middle of it.

We crawled back until we were out of sight and then got on our horses. Mr. McGee kicked his in the ribs and slashed his rump with the barrel of his gun, and the horse broke into a gallop. I was right behind.

I intended to look for the men I figured were the Indians' captives as we rode through. I hoped the people in the stage station didn't mistake us for Indians and shoot us down. We were a pretty rough looking pair but probably recognizable as whites.

Both our horses were tired, and the best they could manage was a lope. We should have stayed out of sight and walked them to within three hundred yards, but that would have been too tame for Mr. McGee. Anyway, both horses were getting tired by the time we got to within three hundred yards of the building.

It wasn't a soddy like the last one we'd stopped at. This one was built out of rough-sawed boards, probably freighted here by the stage company. It was a big, comfortable-looking building that probably had rooms for travelers and served them meals. A few puffs of smoke showed in the windows of the place, and I held my breath for fear one of those inside might be shooting at us.

Off to one side, as we pounded between two concealed groups of Indians, I heard a white man shout, "Hey! Over here! For the love of God. . . ."

I thought he had a gall talking about God after what he and his friends had done. I looked for him but I couldn't see him and I sure wasn't going to slow down for a better look.

We reached the stage station, but just as we did, my horse took a bullet in the rump. His hind legs went out from under him and he fell, rolling and throwing me clear. I thought I'd broken my neck but I managed to hold onto my gun. As soon as I'd quit rolling I jumped to my feet and sprinted for the door, which someone was holding open for me. Mr. McGee had already disappeared inside.

After being outside, it was pretty dark and it took me a minute to get my eyes used to it. When they did, I saw eight people. Three of the men were at the windows, shooting at the Indians. All three were bearded and dressed in working clothes. I guessed they were probably the driver of the coach sitting beside the corral, and maybe the guard and the operator of the stage station.

Besides these three there was an Army captain, in his blue uniform. There was a middle-aged woman I supposed might be the wife of the stage-station operator, an elderly man, and, of all people, Miss Amy Hunnicutt. There was another woman, older and very pretty, who might have been a saloon woman, though I wasn't much of a judge as to what they were supposed to look like.

The captain seemed to be in charge. As soon as Mr. McGee and I had caught our breath, he asked, "Who are you, and how do you happen to be away out here?"

Mr. McGee stuck out his hand and introduced himself. I shook hands with the captain and he promptly tried to crush my hand. I said, "We were following those Indians."

"Following them?" He sounded like he didn't believe me. "What for?"

"They have two captives. The two are killers that we've followed all the way from Illinois."

"For what purpose, may I ask?"

"To kill them," I said.

"Well, there'll be none of that while I'm around."

I said, "Captain, you may not be around for very long. There are twenty or thirty Indians out there." I didn't see any reason in standing there arguing with him. I looked at the middle-aged woman. "Ma'am, have you got anything to eat? We haven't had anything today and not much yesterday."

"Of course. You just come with me." She headed for the kitchen and I followed her.

Amy Hunnicutt apparently hadn't recognized me. She said, "Maybe I can help."

"Of course you can." The woman smiled and the girl flushed, and the four of us went to the kitchen.

I couldn't take my eyes off the girl. She was even prettier than I remembered her.

18

The woman who helped her husband with the way station was Mrs. Roark, a thick, smiling, Irish woman who laid out a feast for us in less than ten minutes. She poured me a cup of steaming black coffee. I was hungry enough so that I didn't even look up until I'd half cleaned up the plate. When I did, Mrs. Roark was watching me approvingly, paying no attention to Mr. McGee. Amy was watching me too, and her eyes looked quickly away when I glanced at her and her face got pink. I said, "I'm Jason Willard. I guess you don't remember me."

Her eyes widened. I could see that finally she did.

"You finally heading west?"

"Yes. We sold the store."

I said, "You'll be out in California all by yourself."

"It will be all right." She said it firmly but her eyes said she was half scared to death at the thought.

I went back to eating. Between bites I talked to Amy Hunnicutt, about her home in Missouri, about her experiences so far on the road, about the people in the other room. The captain, she said, was Captain Walt, headed for duty at Fort Laramie. The woman was Miss Honey Ballantyne, and she was an actress heading for San Francisco, or maybe she'd stop in Denver if she liked it well enough. The coach driver was named Cheyenne Duggins, and the guard was Pete Hanrahan.

Amy Hunnicutt talked a blue streak. She had a fine flush on her cheeks and an excited shine in her eyes, and I knew she was mighty glad to have someone her own age to talk to for a change. Her father came to the door, saw her talking to me and frowned, but he withdrew without saying anything.

Meantime, the Indians outside kept on plinking away at the windows of the stage station, and once I heard glass break and someone curse. Mr. McGee sat all this time, watching me and Amy Hunnicutt without saying anything. I caught his glance once and shook my head faintly to let him know he was to stay away from her. If he was looking for a showdown with me, the best way to get it was to start messing around with this girl. I didn't figure she was mine by any means, but she was too damned nice for Mr. McGee.

When we had finished eating, we went back into the big stagecoach waiting room. There didn't seem to be any urgency, and no decisions to be made about anything, and besides the captain seemed to be in charge. I sat down in one of the leather-covered sofas and began to whittle a toothpick. Amy Hunnicutt sat down at my side. She seemed to like me, and that was fine because I'd sure taken a shine to her.

The captain scowled and came over and stood looking down at me. "Is that all you plan to do, young man? Just sit there and pick your teeth? Get over there to the window and let's see if you're as good with that gun as the way you wear it makes you out to be."

I said, "Captain, I'm not in your army, so don't give me orders. Besides that, this gun hasn't got enough range to do those Indians any harm. I'd just be wasting ammunition."

The captain's face got pretty red. His eyes narrowed. I was glad I wasn't in his army and under his command. He said, "Young man, I am in charge here! You will do what I tell you to."

Amy Hunnicutt was sitting perched on the edge of the couch. Her face was white. I said, "Captain, you're upsetting this lady. Go shoot out the window yourself if it will make you feel any better." I'd never talked to an adult that way before in all my life. It wasn't the way I'd been raised. But I'd been growing up mighty fast in the last few months, and besides that, the captain was a pompous ass.

He glared at me as if he'd like to kill me then and there, but there wasn't anything he could do short of yanking me up and either hitting or spanking me. I guess he decided he didn't really want to try doing either one.

He ended up turning and stalking away. I glanced at Amy, and she was looking at me the way I'd always hoped a girl would look at me some day.

Mr. Roark came over and sat down next to me. He was a weathered, dried up man, but looking at him I guessed he was tough enough for the job he held. He said, "Whew! What did you say to him?"

"Said I wasn't in his army and wouldn't take orders from him." I was embarrassed by the subject so I changed it. "What are these Indians attacking this place for? Are they after the horses in the corral?" I'd about decided they couldn't just be after the horses or they'd have ridden in and got them a long time before now. Doing that wasn't any more risky than shooting up the stage station.

Roark shook his head. "Ain't that. They just plain hate white people and want to kill as many of them as they can. Couple of years ago a Colonel of Volunteers name of Chivington jumped a Cheyenne village on Sand Creek and wiped it out. Killed near four hundred of them, including women and kids. Since then hardly a stagecoach gets through that don't get attacked."

"How long you think they'll stay out there?"

"I figure they're waitin' for reinforcements. Or else they'll try to rush this place just before dark."

"Why not during the night?"

"Indians don't like to fight at night. I've heard it's somethin' about what happens to the soul of a man killed at night."

"What if we keep on holding them off? Will they eventually go away?"

"If we can hurt 'em enough, they will. Soon as they

figure their medicine is bad, they'll quit. But we haven't hurt 'em at all so far."

"When did they attack?"

"Early this morning, just after the stage came in. I was out in the corral hitchin' up the fresh teams. A couple of horses are still standin' there with parts of the harness on 'em."

He looked at me, and then, surprisingly, he said, "What do *you* think we ought to do?"

I said, "Me? I don't know anything about Indians."

"But you look like you knew what you was doing, for all you ain't much more'n a boy."

Well now, I'd be a liar if I said that didn't please me. I said, "If they'll only go away if we hurt 'em enough, then I guess we ought to hurt them all we can. Trouble is, it's like I told the captain. They're too far away for me to hurt them with this gun."

"I've got a rifle you can use."

"All right." I glanced at Mr. McGee. I could see he was irritated because the man had consulted me instead of him. Pretty soon Roark came back with a nice Henry rifle, the repeating kind. He handed it to me and showed me how to use it. I smiled at Amy Hunnicutt and went to one of the windows.

Out there somewhere were the two men who had killed my folks. I didn't have to worry about them anymore, because it was a cinch the Indians weren't going to let them go. They'd be killed, probably in a way that would take a while, if all the stories I had heard were true.

Outside everything was orange from the glow of the setting sun. I couldn't see anything. I rested the rifle on the sill of the broken window and waited. Pretty soon an Indian raised up to take a shot at the building and I was ready for him. I fired and he jerked erect, threw out his arms, and fell back. Over at the other window Cheyenne Duggins bawled, "Nice shootin', son."

The death of the Indian didn't set too well with the others. They all reared up and began shooting. A bullet took some glass out of the window over my head, and pieces of glass came down and cut my face, but I had a bead on another Indian and I fired before I took notice of the cuts. This Indian doubled over forward like he had stomach cramps and disappeared behind a clump of brush.

A dozen or so Indians jumped up from the brush clumps and rocks behind which they'd hid themselves, and came charging toward the stage station. It was reckless and suicidal and didn't make much sense, but I'd hurt them by killing two of their number and I guess they thought they had to try getting even.

Over at one of the other windows, Duggins' gun was firing, and at the other window, Hanrahan was shooting as fast as he could. The Indians zigzagged from side to side trying to throw off our aim, but I got one and saw another go down. One was only shot in the leg, and he got up and crow-hopped back to safety. I knocked a third one down, and either Hanrahan or Duggins got a fourth. Those that were left decided right then they didn't want to come any farther. They veered away to both sides, and even though we tried hitting them, all of us missed.

The flurry of action was over as quickly as it had started, but by now all the orange glow had faded from the sky and land, and everything was gray. I didn't figure the Indians would try again if they were as fussy as Roark had said about dying at night.

Behind me I suddenly became aware that Amy Hunnicutt was crying. I leaned the rifle against the wall. Mr. McGee came quickly to take my place and I went to her. She was down on the floor beside her father.

His face was gray and twisted as if he was in awful pain. He seemed to be having trouble breathing. His eyes looked up at her as if, suddenly, he realized that he was leaving her all alone in a strange and hostile land.

Then his face relaxed and his chest was still, and his hand, which had been clutching hers, went limp. She let out an awful cry and buried her face in his chest.

Everybody just stood around, their faces grave, waiting for her weeping to subside. When it finally did, Mrs. Roark, and Honey Ballantyne got on either side and lifted her up. She turned toward Mrs. Roark, and Honey Ballantyne let her go. Amy and Mrs. Roark went over and sat down on a couch.

Mr. Hunnicutt was dead. I helped, and we lifted him and carried him into one of the rooms provided for overnight stagecoach passengers.

It was completely dark inside the stage station by now. The only light was the last gray in the sky coming through the shattered windows. Nobody said anything about lighting lamps. The captain, plainly trying to regain his command of the situation, said, "Don't anybody light any lamps or strike any matches. Maybe they won't fight at night, but that don't mean they won't shoot if we give them something to shoot at."

Nobody had intended lighting lamps anyway, so that was unnecessary. Honey Ballantyne began to cry, and Mr. McGee went over and sat down on the sofa with her and began to talk to her. I grinned a little to myself, figuring that before half an hour had passed he'd have her in one of the rooms. I didn't care, though, because she wasn't spoken for and wouldn't get him into any fights.

I sat down by myself in the darkness in a spot from which I could see the windows. I had my revolver and I knew if they came through the windows I could get five of them. But I didn't think they'd come.

19

The Indians did not attack. For a long time nothing happened at all. Mr. McGee and Honey Ballantyne talked in lowered tones, and it was a sure bet he'd have her in one of the rooms soon.

Before long, I saw them get up from the sofa and disappear, and a little later, the captain said, "They're building fires. What the hell. . . ."

I went to one of the windows. Cheyenne Duggins was there, peering out. The Indians seemed to have plenty of firewood. It looked to me like they had taken poles from the corral and broken them up.

They built two fires, big ones, both just out of effective rifle range. Then they dragged their two captives out. They stripped them naked, with the captives fighting all the time. When that was done, they tied them to corral poles that had been sunk into the ground. The captives were facing the way station, naked as the day they were born.

Mrs. Roark got up, took one look, and turned away. Amy Hunnicutt didn't look. She was pale and she was weeping. Mrs. Roark sat down beside her again. Mrs. Roark knew what was going to happen and I figured I did too.

I didn't give a damn what the Indians did to their two captives. I'd followed them more than a thousand miles, to kill them myself. But I couldn't have devised a more painful way for them to die. Most satisfying to me was what they were going through now, waiting for it to begin. Maybe dreading what they knew was going to happen was even worse than having it happen.

An Indian took a flaming stick out of the fire. He carried it to one of the captives and stood in front of him, waving the burning stick. Then he stood utterly motionless for several minutes. When he moved, even before he touched his victim with the flame, the man was screaming. When the fire touched his belly, the scream rose in pitch, wavering, rising, and falling. The Indian stepped away and the screams died to groans.

Cheyenne Duggins began firing. The dust his bullets kicked up was well short of the fires. He elevated his rifle barrel and kept firing but he didn't hit anything. I put a hand on his arm and said, "Let it be. You can't hit them anyway and you're wasting ammunition."

"I've got to try. Them murderin' heathen devils. . . !"

I said, "I know the men they've got tied to those stakes. They murdered my mother and father and left me for dead. They didn't just kill my mother, either. They. . . ." I couldn't go on.

Duggins stopped firing and turned his head. He stared at me. I got control of myself and said, "I've followed them all the way from Illinois. I'd have killed them myself if I'd caught them before the Indians did. So don't waste any sympathy on them. What they're getting is less than they deserve."

He got up from the window. "Well, I can't watch. They're human, no matter what they've done."

I didn't much want to watch either. It was sickening. It made my stomach churn and made me want to throw up. It made me hate Indians worse than I hated the men they were torturing.

But I couldn't pull myself away. I had to watch. I had to know what finally happened to the pair. I owed my folks that much.

Another Indian got himself a flaming torch. He carried it to the second man. The man began begging at the top of his lungs even before he was touched. I couldn't tell the two apart, the distance was so great, but this one looked smaller than the others and I supposed it was the sallow-faced kid. The Indian stood in front of him for several minutes, threatening him with the torch. Long before he touched him with it, the kid was screaming. The Indian continued to burn him until the kid sagged against the ropes that bound him to the stake.

By now, Mrs. Roark was white-faced with shock. Amy Hunnicutt was weeping hysterically. I got up and went to Mrs. Roark. "Get something to put in her ears. This is going to go on for a long time yet."

She nodded without speaking. She disappeared and came back shortly with some cotton, which she gave to Amy Hunnicutt to put into her ears. I'd been sitting on the sofa with my arm around Amy while Mrs. Roark was gone. When I got up, she looked at me, her eyes brimming with tears. She began to shake and Mrs. Roark put her arm around her and began to talk soothingly to her. Poor Amy, I thought. It was just too much to lose her father and have this happen in the same night.

I returned to the window. The captain came over and stooped to peer out. His face was pale. He said savagely, "The murderin' devils! They're not human. They're animals!"

I said, "Captain, the men they're torturing are worse. The Indians are getting even for something white men did to two of their women. Those men they've got tied up, they kill for the fun of it. Or for a few dollars. Or for no reason at all."

"You know them?"

"I know them."

"Well, this is barbarous!" One of the Indians now approached the first man, who was still conscious. I saw the firelight gleam on the blade of a knife.

I knew what he was going to do. I turned away, the man's screams of agony filling my ears. I picked up the Henry rifle Roark had given me. Kneeling, I rested the barrel on the window frame. I sighted, fired, raised my sights, and fired again. I emptied the gun but I didn't hit anything. It was just too far.

I put the gun aside. I couldn't watch while the Indians revived and worked on the other one with their knives. The next time I did look, both of the captives had passed out and were slumped against the ropes that tied them to the stakes.

I heard a door close and turned my head. In the faint light thrown into the room by the Indians' fires I saw Mr. McGee and Honey Ballantyne coming out of the room they'd gone into earlier. The captain barked, "Where the hell have you two been?"

Mr. McGee snapped back, "What the hell business is it of yours? I'm not in your damned army. I'll thank you to remember it."

The two faced each other, and I wondered if it was going to result in a fight. It didn't, though. They glared at each other for a while and then both of them turned away.

Out by the fires, the Indians were trying to revive their prisoners. They threw water on them but it was a while before the captives began to revive. I found myself hoping they'd go too far next time and kill both men. Then the ordeal of having to listen to those bloodcurdling screams would be over with.

Mr. McGee came over to the window, hunkered down, and stared out. I didn't look at him or speak to him. In my opinion, the business with Honey Ballantyne was pretty bad, particularly when men were being tortured within sight and hearing of both of them.

He asked, "What's the matter with you?" His tone was defiant.

I turned my head and looked him straight in the eye. I said, "I'm disgusted with you, that's all."

"For what?"

"For hauling that saloon girl off into the bedroom while those men were screaming out there."

"Well, ain't you the prissy one!" He put all the contempt he could into his voice. "You sound like you cared what happens to that pair."

"I just think some things are decent and some aren't, that's all."

"And the things I do aren't, is that it?"

I thought, Here it comes, but I wouldn't lie about the way I felt to avoid a showdown with him. It was coming anyway, and I guessed now was as good a time as any. I said, "I guess that's about it."

"Damn you. . . ." He got to his feet. I stood up facing him. The light from the Indians' fires highlighted his face and made him look different. One of his eyes, the one toward the fires, seemed to have a glow all its own.

I realized how tense I was, half crouched, my right arm partly bent, my hand like a claw only a couple of inches from the grips of my gun. I wasn't afraid. I knew that if Mr. McGee grabbed for his gun he was a dead man. I would kill him before he could draw his gun and get it up into line. I knew how fast he was and I knew how fast I was, and I guess he did too because I saw the beginning of a little hesitation in his face.

The captain yelled shrilly, "What the hell? Are you two fighting?" and came hurrying toward us.

I said, "Stay out of it, Captain. It's none of your affair."

I heard a woman gasp, but I didn't take my eyes off Mr. McGee. I could hear the captain's footsteps approaching, aware that if he barged into this, he could sure as hell change the outcome of it.

Mr. McGee suddenly relaxed. He turned his head. "It's all right, Captain. Nothing's happening."

I still didn't take my eyes off him. I was aware that he might be trying to throw me off guard so that he could draw and kill me without getting killed himself. But I guess that wasn't in his mind. He turned and crossed the room toward Honey Ballantyne.

I felt myself go limp. I was sweating and my hands were clammy. That had been the closest we'd ever come.

20

Glancing outside, I saw that the Indians had succeeded in reviving their prisoners. For a while, they were content to threaten them, but so convincing were their threats that every time one of them came near, the captives would begin yelling and begging for mercy again.

I was getting sick, so I forced myself to think of my folks. I wondered if my mother had begged them for mercy. If she had, it hadn't done her any good, and begging these savages for mercy wasn't going to do her murderers any good.

Listening to the people behind me, I knew they couldn't stand much more. Amy Hunnicutt was weeping again despite the cotton in her ears, which couldn't be altogether effective. Mrs. Roark had put cotton into her own ears. She wasn't weeping but she was very pale and her face was drawn with strain.

The captain was pacing back and forth, scowling and muttering to himself. Mr. McGee had his arm around Honey Ballantyne, but she suddenly threw it off and got to her feet. "Damn you, stop pawing me! Get away from me! Get clear away!"

Mr. McGee sat dumfounded on the sofa, so Honey Ballantyne rushed away from him. I studied Mr. McGee's face. The only light was from the fires but it was enough to see the way he looked.

His face was dark with fury. Twice now in the space of a few minutes, he had been humiliated, first by having to back down from me, the second time by being rejected by Honey Ballantyne.

He caught me looking at him and his face became even more furious. I didn't want to look away but I forced myself to, knowing that if I didn't, he'd think he was backed into a corner and forced to challenge me again.

I'd felt a lot of things toward Mr. McGee, but I'd never felt pity for him like I did right now. It must be terrible, I thought, to have to prove your courage and manhood over and over again, every day of your life.

I wondered what he would do. Something, certainly. He had no other choice, being what he was. What I was sure of was that he wouldn't shoot me down without giving me a chance.

Over in the corner, Honey Ballantyne suddenly screamed, "Why doesn't somebody do something? Why doesn't somebody go out there and do something?"

A silence followed her outburst, broken by the sudden, piercing screech of pain from one of the Indians' captives outside.

There was a flurry of movement where Mr. McGee had been. I glanced that way and saw that he was on his feet. Gun in hand, he plunged toward the door.

I knew what he was going to do. Once more he was going to prove his manhood—to everyone here, but mostly to himself. I also knew that if he wasn't stopped, this was going to be the last time he'd ever have to prove himself.

Rifle in hand, I ran after him. The door slammed open and he ran outside. I was no more than three or four yards behind as he plunged across the bare yard in front of the stage station toward the fires of the Indians.

I had the Henry rifle in my hand, fully loaded, and my revolver in its holster. Mr. McGee had only his revolver. I opened my mouth to yell at him, then shut it without making a sound. If I yelled, it would only alert the Indians.

Mr. McGee suddenly veered sharply right, perhaps realizing that if the Indians looked up from what they were doing they would surely look toward the stage station. I followed him, running as hard as I'd ever run in my life before. I began to gain on him but so slowly I knew it was not going to be enough. Mr. McGee, knowing I was following, ran like a deer.

For an instant I considered trying to shoot him in the leg and bring him down before he reached the Indians. I discarded the idea almost immediately. I'd have to stop before I'd be sure enough of my aim. And besides, the shot would bring the Indians. We'd both be caught before we could get back to the safety of the stage station.

I considered stopping and letting him go on. But that was also unacceptable. His faults and frailties were clear to me, yet without him I'd have lost the men I had been following. However precarious our friendship had become, Mr. McGee still had a strange hold on me.

So I ran on. Finally, no more than a hundred and fifty feet from the naked captives tied to the stakes, he skidded to a halt, knelt, and raised his revolver with both hands.

He fired, and I saw the smallest of the two captives suddenly slump against his bonds. Instantly the Indians turned, and immediately a howl went up.

Knowing our time was nearly gone, I raised the Henry to my shoulder and put a bullet into the chest of the second man, the one with the blue and penetrating eyes. Reaching down, I yanked Mr. McGee to his feet. "Come on! It's done!"

He broke into a run, with me right beside him. I glanced over my shoulder and saw that the nearest of the Indians were less than twenty feet behind. I slowed enough to turn and put a bullet into the closest one. He seemed to stumble and fall, rolling afterward for several feet.

Turning and shooting had slowed me down, and now Mr. McGee was half a dozen feet ahead. A few shots racketed behind me but neither of us was hit.

From the stage station, I heard a scream. I glanced

that way and saw everybody clustered in the shattered windows, peering out. I didn't know who had screamed, but it didn't matter anyway. What did matter was the sudden effect it had on Mr. McGee.

He yanked himself to a halt, whirled, and dropped to one knee. I bawled, "You damn fool, don't. . . !" But I could just as well have saved my breath. One last time he had to prove himself, and this one was going to cost him his life, and probably was going to cost me mine.

Because I couldn't just run on.

I planted my feet and skidded to a halt. Having been a little behind Mr. McGee before he stopped, I was able to halt almost as quickly as he did. A dozen Indians were bearing down on us, but Mr. McGee's gun was roaring as quickly as he could fire it. I levered the Henry, getting an Indian with nearly every shot, but they didn't stop. A bullet grazed my ribs, bringing the warm wetness of blood immediately afterward, and an Indian I had shot plunged into me, dead when he hit me, but knocking me sprawling for half a dozen feet.

I clawed out from under him. A quick glance showed me that Mr. McGee was down. It also showed me that I was nearly surrounded by Indians. I figured I was a goner too, but if I was going to die, by God I was going to take some of these savages along with me.

I fought to my feet, the Henry still in my hands. Using it as a club, holding it by the barrel, I swung, catching one Indian alongside the head, and bringing him down almost at my feet.

The Henry had been wrenched out of my hands when it connected with his head, so I yanked my revolver from its holster. I heard it firing, more rapidly than I had ever heard a gun fired before, and I saw the Indians falling before me as if they had been struck by some kind of divine retribution and not simply by bullets from my gun.

In an instant, there were six dead Indians not six

feet from where I stood. The others, behind them, suddenly stopped their headlong rush toward me. Smoke rose from the muzzle of my gun, stinging my nostrils. It seemed like an eternity that the Indians and I faced each other over the pile of dead Indians.

Then, so suddenly that it left me weak, the Indians turned to right and left and disappeared. I remembered what somebody had said about their quitting when they figured their medicine is bad. They could have killed me with ease, because both my guns were empty and I was defenseless. Instead, they had withdrawn.

I didn't waste any time trying to figure it out. I shoved the revolver back into its holster and grabbed Mr. McGee under the arms. I dragged him toward the stage way station, and Roark and Duggins came out to give me a hand. We reached the door and carried Mr. McGee inside and laid him on the couch. Mrs. Roark knelt at his side and felt his throat for pulse. She got up, looking at me and shaking her head.

So Mr. McGee was dead. So were the men I had trailed so far. My quest was over and I suddenly felt drained.

I stood there looking down at Mr. McGee and I felt tears sting my eyes. No longer would he need to atone for his moment of cowardice during the war. No longer would he need to prove himself.

I felt a timid hand on my arm and I turned my head. Amy Hunnicutt stood beside me, looking up into my face. Her face was pale and streaked with tears and she was looking at me with the compassion of one who knew exactly how I felt.

I knew, then, that this was not the end. I would put my gun away. I would go on, to Denver City, with Amy Hunnicutt. She was alone, and I was alone, but being alone is only a temporary thing. I put my hand on hers and turned away from the body lying on the couch. It was time to begin anew.

Lewis B. Patten wrote more than ninety Western novels in thirty years and three of them won Spur Awards from the Western Writers of America and the author himself the Golden Saddleman Award. Indeed, this highlights the most remarkable aspect of his work: not that there is so much of it, but that so much of it is so fine. Patten was born in Denver, Colorado, and served in the U.S. Navy 1933–1937. He was educated at the University of Denver during the war years and became an auditor for the Colorado Department of Revenue during the 1940s. It was in this period that he began contributing significantly to Western pulp magazines, fiction that was from the beginning fresh and unique and revealed Patten's lifelong concern with the sociological and psychological effects of group psychology on the frontier. He became a professional writer at the time of his first novel, *Massacre at White River* (1952). The dominant theme in much of his fiction is the notion of justice, and its opposite, injustice. In his first novel it has to do with exploitation of the Ute Indians, but as he matured as a writer he explored this theme with significant and poignant detail in small towns throughout the early West. Crimes, such as rape or lynching, were often at the centre of his stories. When the values embodied in these small towns are examined closely, they are found to be wanting. Conformity is always easier than taking a stand. Yet, in Patten's view of the American West, there is usually a man or a woman who refuses to conform. Among his finest titles, always a difficult choice, surely are *A Killing at Kiowa* (1972), *Ride a Crooked Trail* (1976), and his many fine contributions to Doubleday's Double D series, including *Villa's Rifles* (1977), *The Law at Cottonwood* (1978), and *Death Rides a Black Horse* (1978). His later books include *Tincup in the Storm Country* (1996), *Trail to Vicksburg* (1997), *Death Rides the Denver Stage* (1999), and *The Woman at Ox-Yoke* (2000).